Disneynature
chimpanzee

Editorial Director: Wendy Lefkon
Associate Editor: Jessica Ward

Illustrated by Jean-Paul Orpiñas
Designed by Stuart Smith

Photography credits:
Ed Anderson: 15, 24 (middle), 29, 30 (top), 33, 52 (top right), 53 (bottom middle),
73 (top right), 74, 75 (bottom middle, top middle, top right), 95, 98, 102 (left), 103
Christophe Boesch: 16, 17, 86 (left)
Genevieve Campbell: 64, 65 (top right, bottom left), 66
Martyn Colbeck: 25 (middle), 51, 61 (top right), 100–101
Mark Linfield: 30 (bottom), 36, 42, 44, 45, 48–49, 53 (top left),
54 (middle), 80 (top left), 104–105
Lydia Luncz: 75 (top left, bottom left, bottom right)
Sonja Metzger: 13, 39, 52 (bottom left), 53 (bottom right), 54 (top left), 63
Kristin Mosher: 12, 19, 26 (middle), 27 (left), 55, 56, 58–59, 61 (bottom), 62, 69,
70, 72, 73 (top left), 87, 107, 108–109, 110 (top), 112–113, 114, 115, 116, 119, 120
Mark van Heukelum (IBREAM): 65 (top left, bottom right)

Maps drawn by Ed Anderson: 22, 23

ISBN 978-1-4231-5364-1

F322-8368-0-12032

First Edition

10 9 8 7 6 5 4 3 2 1

Printed in the United States of America

Disney nature
chimpanzee
THE MAKING OF THE FILM

BY

CHRISTOPHE BOESCH
AND SANJIDA O'CONNELL

WITH

ED ANDERSON,
MARTYN COLBECK,
ALASTAIR FOTHERGILL,
MARK LINFIELD,
JOHN MITANI,
KRISTIN MOSHER,
JAMES REED,
AND BILL WALLAUER

FOREWORD BY
JANE GOODALL

DISNEY
EDITIONS
NEW YORK

Contents

*I*n 1961, when working for a Ph.D. in ethology at Cambridge in England, I was told I should have given the chimpanzees numbers—not names—and that I could not talk about them having personalities, minds, or emotions. Those concepts applied only to humans. Fortunately though, I had not been to college, so I had never heard this. And I had a wonderful teacher all through childhood who taught me that this was not true—my dog Rusty!

It was because chimpanzees are so very like us in their biology and in so many aspects of their behavior that it was possible to influence the scientific thinking of the time. Today, most field researchers name the animals they are studying, especially if they are primates. And in major universities around the world, one can take courses about animal minds, animal emotions, and even animal personalities.

Of course, the best way to learn about chimpanzees and their behavior is to watch them in their natural habitat in Africa. But most people will never have the opportunity. It is for this reason that films of wild chimpanzees are so important.

The footage obtained by Hugo van Lawick for the National Geographic Society not only helped other scientists appreciate what I was reporting from what is today Gombe National Park in Tanzania, but also introduced the Gombe chimpanzees to the general public around the world.

Today, cinematography has advanced and new technologies have made the equipment more efficient in the dim lighting of the forest. But it has not made the task of the camera crew any easier as they work in sometimes extremely challenging environments. I hope that everyone who sees *Chimpanzee* will appreciate the extraordinary physical effort that went into making the film.

Chimpanzee will bring chimpanzees and the excitements and tragedies of their forest world into the hearts of people everywhere. I hope it will encourage more people to help try to protect our relatives for otherwise they face extinction. Their numbers are shrinking in the face of human population growth, habitat destruction, and the threat posed by the bushmeat trade—the commercial hunting of wild animals for food.

Creating protected areas is not enough. We must also work to improve the lives of the people living in and around the last great forests, try to alleviate the crippling poverty in so many villages, and help the people find alternative livelihoods to charcoal burning and hunting. The local people become our partners in conservation. And we must introduce education programs for the people in the cities, as well as those living in and around chimpanzee habitats.

The Jane Goodall Institute's community-centered conservation program —TACARE—has led to the restoration of forest around Gombe National Park and the protection of a forested chimpanzee habitat in a huge area to the south. The program has been successfully replicated in the Democratic Republic of the Congo (DRC), Uganda, and Guinea. In addition, a variety of conservation organizations are undertaking initiatives to help people in order to protect the last chimpanzee populations in other countries. One example is Christophe Boesch's Wild Chimpanzee Foundation, which focuses on conservation, research, and education.

Finally, the Institute's sanctuary for orphan chimpanzees, whose mothers have been killed for meat, is serving as an education center to help local people—especially children—learn about their extraordinary chimpanzee neighbors. After a visit, the local people say they will never harm chimpanzees again.

Jane Goodall, Ph.D., DBE
Founder, the Jane Goodall Institute & UN Messenger of Peace
janegoodall.org

The male is huge, grizzled, the hair on his broad back white with age. Freddy is the leader of the troop, known for his ability to wage war on his enemies and keep his group under control. And yet in spite of this he extends one hand toward the baby chimpanzee. Oscar is, at first, wary. He's only three years old. He's lost his mother and has no one to turn to. Freddy moves and picks up a stone. With considerable force, he smashes it down on a nut. The shell cracks open, and Freddy offers the kernel to Oscar. The little chimp takes the nut and eats it with relish. It's the first food Oscar's eaten for a long while. Freddy cracks open another nut. Oscar edges closer until he's sitting right next to the big male. He rests one hand on Freddy's knee. The alpha male, when he's cracked enough nuts to take the edge off Oscar's hunger, leans over and tenderly grooms the baby, his hands enormous against the little chimp.

It's midday and hot. Freddy takes a break from nut cracking and rests in the shade. He pulls the orphan tightly to his chest, hugging him closely as if to try and make up for the loss of his mother. Instead of sleeping, the tiny chimp stares into the distance, a faint glimmer of anxiety in his eyes, hoping perhaps that this will last, that the big male will feed him and care for him— that Freddy will become his new father.

Part One

CHIMPANZEES (*PAN TROGLODYTES*)

Wild chimpanzees, which are endangered, live in complex social groups of 15–150 individuals in African forests. They're omnivorous: they eat a wide range of fruit, foliage, mushrooms, honey, and insects, and they hunt monkeys, bushpigs, and antelopes for meat. Chimps are similar to us in height and weight—adults are 4 to 5.5 feet tall and weigh between 70 and 130 pounds. Although they are our closest living relative, sharing 98 percent of our genes, their brains are much smaller than ours; while an adult human brain weighs just under three pounds, a chimp's weighs about a third of that: ten to sixteen ounces. Chimps are long-lived, reaching forty-five years old. Males are classed as adults at fifteen, and females can give birth at thirteen. Like us, chimpanzees have opposable thumbs and are highly dexterous. They make and use tools—they fish for termites with sticks, use leaves as sponges, and crack nuts with stone or wooden hammers.

Why Chimpanzees?

On Earth Day—April 22, 2009—the first film under the Disneynature banner, *Earth*, debuted in theaters nationwide across North America. Directed by Alastair Fothergill and Mark Linfield, *Earth* marked the official launch of Disneynature, the first new Disney-branded film label introduced by The Walt Disney Company in more than sixty years. In the tradition of Walt Disney's classic wildlife films, True-Life Adventures, which were produced from 1948 to 1960, Disneynature endeavors to bring the remarkable stories of the natural world to life on the big screen. "I think audiences worldwide are really looking for films that are entertaining, beautiful, educational, and environmentally conscious," says Jean-Francois Camilleri, General Manager of Disneynature.

Following the success of *Earth*, Jean-Francois invited the filmmakers to come up with another wildlife feature film with a great story. The challenge was to find a subject that could hold people's attention for eighty minutes in a movie theater and be emotionally engaging enough to make people laugh or cry—ideally both. Mark and Alastair thought that chimpanzees had that potential.

Chimpanzees are our closest living relatives; our common ancestor lived four to eight million years ago (see "Chimpanzees" sidebar). Chimps share 98 percent of our genetic code. Biologically, we are so close that we can catch diseases and receive blood transfusions from each other. Perhaps because they're "family," we see ourselves reflected in chimpanzees. Like us, they can walk upright on two legs—although most of the time they travel either on all fours, resting on the knuckles of their hands, or by swinging through the trees. They have many humanlike characteristics: they can use tools, cooperate with one another, hunt, communicate using a wide range of sounds, show both deception and altruism. Like us, they have a tender side and an aggressive streak.

Chimpanzees live in groups with complex social networks; they have friends and enemies. There's a strong mother-infant bond, with offspring relying on their moms for up to ten years. Even more important for a feature film, chimps are characters with their own personality quirks. We can tell individuals apart, and we can guess, from their expressive faces, how they're feeling. "In a shot of a chimpanzee's head and shoulders on a movie screen," Mark Linfield comments, "the eyes will be the size of grapefruits, so you feel as if you can see into their souls. We have an incredible bond with these animals—it's as though you can guess what they might be thinking. It's a connection you experience best by seeing them on the big screen."

Disneynature liked Alastair and Mark's proposal. The question was, which chimpanzees should the directors film for the movie? Most documentaries for television have shown chimps living in open woodland at the edge of the East African savannah. The chimps' ancestral home, however, is the rain forests in the "dark heart of Africa," in the western side of the continent. Chimpanzees are incredibly difficult animals to observe, but there is a population of these apes in the Taï forest—in West Africa's Ivory Coast—that has been studied for over thirty years by Dr. Christophe Boesch, from the Max Planck Institute for Evolutionary Anthropology in Germany, (see "Thirty Years of Taï Chimps" sidebar). The chimpanzees at Taï belong to a subspecies known as the West African chimpanzee. One of the largest populations of this subspecies—consisting of around five hundred chimps—is in Taï National Park. The Taï chimps were accustomed to people following them but had very rarely been filmed, so they seemed like perfect subjects for a movie.

However, Mark and Alastair had filmed in the Taï forest before. Although it was a beautiful forest, the experience had been punishing and both had vowed never to return. Both directors have considerable expertise; as well as making films about chimpanzees, they had worked on landmark natural history series in technically difficult locations ranging from the North Pole to the deep sea. But they had reservations about returning to Taï because of the challenges they would encounter making a movie featuring wild animals in such a remote and difficult location. They decided to go on a reconnaissance trip to see if the Taï forest (see "Taï National Park" sidebar) was as difficult a place for a film crew as they remembered.

— THIRTY YEARS OF TAI CHIMPS —

During World War II, French colonial troops undertook missions deep into the Taï forest in the Ivory Coast. To their astonishment, they heard strange sounds ringing through the jungle. They thought they were hearing undiscovered tribes working with iron, but this theory was unsubstantiated. Decades later, in 1976, similar rumors attracted two young Swiss-French scientists, Christophe Boesch and his wife, Hedwige Boesch-Achermann, to the Ivory Coast. But they were not looking for undiscovered tribes of people . . .

At the time, most academics thought that humans were the only animal on the planet capable of using tools. In the 1960s, primatologist Dr. Jane Goodall was in the process of establishing a long-term study of chimpanzees living on the edge of the savannah in East Africa, and over the next two decades, her

research started to slowly overturn this dogma. But because humans evolved in the savannah, some scientists suggested that chimpanzees living in this same kind of environment might be more like us. No one had studied chimpanzees in their true home, deep in the tropical rain forest, to see if they too used tools.

Christophe had been fascinated by animals since he was seven. As a young man, he decided that he wanted to find a group of chimpanzees to follow; in particular, he wanted to study their tool use. When he and his wife arrived in the Ivory Coast, it seemed as if his dream might come true. As he and Hedwige had hoped, local people told him that the "iron-working tribes" making noise in the forest were actually chimpanzees using tools. Not only that, they said that the chimps used elephant tusks to crack nuts, and that they hunted monkeys, skinning the animals and making their pelts into backpacks for carrying the nuts.

"This sounded too incredible to be true," recalls Christophe. "I wondered, were the Taï chimpanzees redefining what it meant to be human, or were the local people telling tall tales?"

Christophe was to discover that while these tales were indeed exaggerated, elements of them were true.

When they began their chimp project, Christophe and Hedwige were so dedicated that they lived in the rain forest for years, even taking their two small children with them. "I know it sounds crazy, taking newborn babies into the jungle," says Christophe, "but we had been living there for six years, and we knew the forest very well. We were confident it was a safe environment." Unsurprisingly, Hedwige was a little less blasé.

On Hedwige's first day back in the rain forest after the birth of her son Lukas, the young researcher grew anxious. She had left Lukas in the camp with two African assistants while she was following the chimpanzees. After a couple of hours, Hedwige doubled back. She stopped a short distance away from the camp and trained her binoculars

on the house. What she saw was one assistant lying on the ground with Lukas sitting on his stomach, while the other entertained the baby by playing the drums on powdered-milk cans. Satisfied, Hedwige returned to the chimps. Lukas and his sister, Léonore, lived in the jungle with the chimps and their parents until he was six and she was two. Hedwige spent a total of twelve years studying the chimps, but the demands of the family and her increasing involvement in chimpanzee conservation left her with less and less time to spend in the Ivory Coast. Christophe continued their studies without her.

In 2011, after more than thirty years of painstaking observation and research, what Christophe had discovered was nothing short of extraordinary. He had learned that the Taï chimpanzees do indeed use tools, wielding hammers to crack nuts on anvils; they use more tools than savannah-dwelling chimpanzees;

and they cooperate to hunt monkeys, teach their youngsters, and wage commando-style attacks on neighboring groups of chimpanzees. "We have learned that the longer you stay, the more there is to discover about these animals," notes Christophe.

OPPOSITE PAGE, TOP: Christophe tries to work whilst looking after Léonore.

OPPOSITE PAGE, BOTTOM: Lukas helping Christophe film the chimps

ABOVE: Among the researchers and BBC team who filmed the series *Trials of Life*, were Alastair Fothergill (front row in the striped shirt), Christophe Boesch (front row with Léonore on his knee), David Attenborough (back row wearing a blue shirt), and Hedwige Boesch-Achermann (back row with Lukas on her knee).

In March 2008, Christophe, directors Mark and Alastair, and chimp expert and cameraman Bill Wallauer undertook a reconnaissance trip, or "recce," to the Ivory Coast to see whether it would be possible to film in the Taï forest. On day one they woke to almost 100 percent humidity. The camp they were staying in was on the edge of the chimpanzees' territory; the men had to walk three miles through the jungle to find the apes. But before they even caught their first glimpse of the chimpanzees, Mark and Alastair began to remember how difficult it had been to film there.

As they trekked through the jungle, temperatures rose to almost 86°F. It was like exercising in a sauna. All around them were massive trees, many yards in girth, their evergreen leaves blocking out the light. Mark and Alastair edged through a tangle of saplings and wove between vines and lianas with tough, almost unbreakable stems. The forest pulsed, alive with the hum of cicadas and the heavy drone of flies and mosquitoes. Mangabeys—a type of ground-dwelling monkey—raced noisily ahead of them. "I love the fact that everything is crawling with life," says Mark, "but the heat and humidity are difficult." The Taï forest is renowned for its rich diversity of wildlife, but many of the animals, like duikers—tiny antelopes—and pygmy hippos, fled when they heard the men's boots crackle through the dry leaves in the undergrowth.

Overhead, an African crowned eagle sailed on the thermals. Below the tree cover, Mark was concerned about how dark it was—even though the sun was high in the sky. He got out his light meter—a device used by cameramen for measuring light levels. "It was so dim, I struggled to see, and I couldn't get a reading from the light meter at all!" recounts Mark.

Finally, they heard the calls—"pant hoots" and barks—of the chimps ahead of them. As soon as the chimps saw the men, they set off deeper into the rain forest. They appeared to be sauntering, but the men had to run to keep up—not an easy task in such a dense thicket. Mark and Alastair were traveling light, but they could imagine the difficulty of attempting to catch up with the chimpanzees while carrying all the equipment they'd need for filming. Even worse, the fleeting shapes of the chimpanzees ahead of them were black. "It would have been like trying to film shadows within the shadows," says Mark.

An hour and a half later, the chimpanzees stopped, and the four men caught their breath. The chimps had spotted a fig tree laden with cherry-size fruit, and with excited shrieks they raced up the trunk and out across the thickest branches. This presented a rather different problem. "When

choosing locations for filming tree-dwelling animals, we prefer forests that are on hilly terrain; this allows you to film from the ground at the top of a hill straight into the canopy of a tree further down the slope. That way, you are eye-level with an animal in the treetops without having to climb yourself," explains Mark. Unfortunately, the Taï forest is flat. So when the chimpanzees were in the tree, all the men could see was an array of bottoms!

After two days of chasing black chimpanzees through dark forest, with the apes sometimes silhouetted against a white sky as they fed in the trees, the men were exhausted and a little depressed. Bill—who works as a cinematographer for the Jane Goodall Institute filming chimpanzees in Gombe, Tanzania—was concerned about the conditions. Gombe is hillier, and the forest is more open. Alastair was unusually quiet. Mark was also worried about the light levels and the fact that when they had seen the chimpanzees, they were barely interacting with each other—as if no one was on speaking terms. "I had a growing feeling that it was not going to be possible to film enough intriguing behavior to make an eighty-minute film," says Mark. It seemed that the Taï forest was simply too challenging a location for a movie. But the next morning, their third and last day, something happened that made them change their minds. The four filmmakers trudged through the forest for several hours. "I was subdued and dragging my feet," recalls Mark. "I dreaded the feeling of leaving without a clear-cut decision, so we needed our last day to be either a disaster or truly amazing—and I suspected it was going to be a disaster."

Then, in the middle of the morning, they came across a clearing in the jungle created by a fallen tree. There, sitting on the rotten trunk, were over thirty chimpanzees, bathed in soft morning sunshine. The sky was a clear azure. A hornbill flew past, making a breathless cackling call, and the chimps startled a mongoose that fled into the brush. Some of the adults sat in lines of four or five individuals, grooming each other. Others were in splinter groups at the edges of the glade.

"Right in front of me, I could see alliances were being made and friendships reinforced," exclaims Mark. Young chimpanzees were playing king of the castle, running up and down a small termite mound, shrieking with delight as they reached the top of the mound or pushed each other off the summit and into the bushes below. They looked just like a group of children playing in the park. Adolescent males were puffing themselves up and putting on displays of false bravado while the females tried to ignore them. "It was the kind of utopian rain forest scene that wildlife artists paint," states Mark. At that moment, both directors were thinking the same thing: this was it. *Chimpanzee* had to be shot in the Taï forest in the Ivory Coast, West Africa.

PAGE 19: Cameraman Bill Wallauer protecting the camera from the frequent rainfall

The Ivory Coast is in West Africa between Liberia and Ghana. In 1893, it was declared a French colony. It achieved independence in 1960 and has a population today of 21.6 million. French remains the national language. Once a stable country, the Ivory Coast was torn apart by a brutal civil war in 2002. Periods of peace alternated with violence until 2011, when the country became dangerously unstable once more due to the outgoing president's contention of the country's first democratic election. The main export is cocoa; Ivorians also trade coffee, tropical wood, cotton, bananas, pineapples, and palm oil.

IVORY COAST

YAMOUSSOUKRO

GHANA

LIBERIA

ABIDJAN

TAÏ FOREST

MINKEBE

LIBREVILLE

GABON

UGANDA

NGOGO

KENYA

MOROCCO

ALGERIA

LIBYA

EGYPT

MAURITANIA

MALI

NIGER

CHAD

SUDAN

SENEGAL

GUNVEA

BURKINA FASO

BENIN

NIGERIA

COTE D'IVOIRE

GHANA TOGO

CAMEROON

CAR

GABON

DEMOCRATIC REPUBLIC of CONGO

UGANDA

CONGO

TANZAN

ANGOLA

ZAMBIA

22

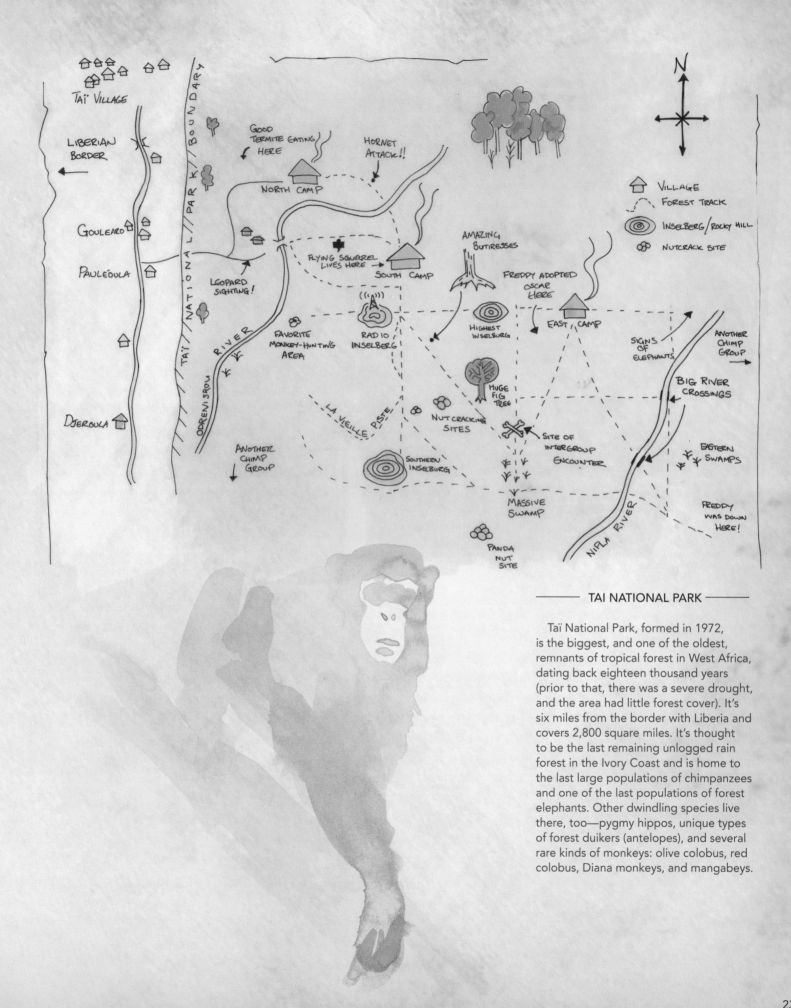

TAÏ VILLAGE

LIBERIAN BORDER

GOULÉARO

PAULÉOULA

DJÉROULA

TAÏ NATIONAL PARK BOUNDARY

ODRÉNI SROU RIVER

GOOD TERMITE EATING HERE

HORNET ATTACK!!

NORTH CAMP

FLYING SQUIRREL LIVES HERE

LEOPARD SIGHTING!

SOUTH CAMP

AMAZING BUTTRESSES

FREDDY ADOPTED OSCAR HERE

FAVORITE MONKEY-HUNTING AREA

RADIO INSELBERG

HIGHEST INSELBURG

EAST CAMP

SIGNS OF ELEPHANTS

ANOTHER CHIMP GROUP

BIG RIVER CROSSINGS

HUGE FIG TREE

LA VIEILLE PISTE

NUTCRACKING SITES

SITE OF INTERGROUP ENCOUNTER

EASTERN SWAMPS

ANOTHER CHIMP GROUP

SOUTHERN INSELBERG

MASSIVE SWAMP

NIFLA RIVER

FREDDY WAS DOWN HERE!

PANDA NUT SITE

VILLAGE
FOREST TRACK
INSELBERG/ROCKY HILL
NUTCRACK SITE

N

TAÏ NATIONAL PARK

Taï National Park, formed in 1972, is the biggest, and one of the oldest, remnants of tropical forest in West Africa, dating back eighteen thousand years (prior to that, there was a severe drought, and the area had little forest cover). It's six miles from the border with Liberia and covers 2,800 square miles. It's thought to be the last remaining unlogged rain forest in the Ivory Coast and is home to the last large populations of chimpanzees and one of the last populations of forest elephants. Other dwindling species live there, too—pygmy hippos, unique types of forest duikers (antelopes), and several rare kinds of monkeys: olive colobus, red colobus, Diana monkeys, and mangabeys.

Ed Anderson
Logistics Manager

Christophe Boesch
Evolutionary Biologist

Martyn Colbeck
Cameraman – Ivory Coast

Originally an expedition leader, Ed would take groups into remote regions in several continents to carry out biodiversity surveys in rain forests. He also had a brief sojourn as a tree surgeon. Ed was hired as the logistics manager for the feature film and was in charge of building a camp in the forest and communicating in French with the local staff. In addition, Ed became Martyn's camera assistant, recorded part of the sound track for the movie, and shot some of the footage for the documentary on the making of *Chimpanzee*.

Ed discovered that even his tree surgery skills had not prepared him for the construction of a platform fifty yards up in the forest canopy next to an eagle's nest.

A French-Swiss biologist, Christophe became the director of the Max Planck Institute for Evolutionary Anthropology, in Leipzig, Germany, in 1997. He first visited the Ivory Coast and studied the Taï chimpanzees in 1976. In 1979, he founded an ongoing long-term project in the Taï forest. He researches the chimpanzees' social organization, tool use, hunting, cooperation, food sharing, intercommunity relationships— and intelligence. He's published many papers and books. His latest book is *Wild Cultures: A Comparison Between Chimpanzee and Human Cultures*. Concerned about the continuing deforestation in Africa, Christophe founded the Wild Chimpanzee Foundation in 2000 (www.wildchimps.org) to fight for the chimps' survival. Hedwige, his wife, says that Christophe has an uncanny ability to predict what the chimpanzees will do when he's following them in the forest.

Martyn is an award-winning filmmaker and photographer who has been filming wildlife all over the world for more than twenty years, working mainly with the BBC's Natural History Unit, in Bristol, England. Martyn filmed sequences for the BBC series *Trials of Life, The Life of Mammals*, and *Planet Earth*. He is best known for his work with African elephants. Of the five elephant films he has made, three have been in collaboration with Cynthia Moss from the Amboseli Trust for Elephants in Kenya. Together, over a period of fifteen years, Martyn and Cynthia chronicled the life of an elephant family led by a matriarch known as Echo. Martyn is partial to a glass or two of wine whether he's on a shoot or not.

Alastair Fothergill
Director

Alastair is an award-winning natural history producer and director. He joined the BBC in 1983 and made a number of films with Sir David Attenborough, including *Life in the Freezer* and *Trials of Life*. He was head of the BBC's Natural History Unit from 1992 to 1998. He stepped down to produce the landmark, award-winning series *The Blue Planet*. This led to his productions of *Planet Earth* and the seven-part series *Frozen Planet*. Alastair has directed three feature films: *Earth* (a global box-office hit), *Deep Blue*, and *African Cats*. Alastair shot his famous film about chimpanzees, *Too Close for Comfort*, in the Taï forest and has loved chimpanzees ever since.

Mark Linfield
Director

Mark has been passionate about nature and photography since he was a child. He first worked for the BBC more than twenty years ago, on a documentary about gorillas living in the Congo. Since the early nineties, he's made a number of award-winning films about monkeys and apes, such as *Temple Troop* and *Orangutans: The High Society*. In 2000, Mark returned to the BBC Natural History Unit to direct the BAFTA-nominated *Life of Mammals* with Sir David Attenborough before going on to direct *Capuchins: The Monkey Puzzle* and two episodes of the multi-Emmy-winning series *Planet Earth*. Mark directed the highly successful *Earth* with Alastair Fothergill. Alongside directing *Chimpanzee*, Mark produced *Frozen Planet*, the sequel to *Planet Earth*. Mark used to be skinny until he discovered and removed several parasitic worms living in his gut, one of which he keeps preserved as a memento in a jar of vodka.

Kristin Mosher
Sound Recordist and
Stills Photographer

Kristin is an award-winning wildlife photographer and sound recordist. With a strong background in science, photography, and physical fitness, Kristin has the ideal attributes required for documenting chimpanzee behavior. As a sound recordist, she has worked on films about chimpanzees in both Tanzania and Uganda. Her photographic work has been used in many publications, including *National Geographic* and *BBC Wildlife Magazine*, as well as numerous books. She was an instrumental part of the *Chimpanzee* team, acting as the key sound recordist and still photographer for the project. Her favorite sound is chimp laughter.

James Reed
Field Producer

Bill Wallauer
Cameraman – Uganda

Liz Stevens
Production Manager

For the last ten years, James has been involved in making factual documentaries, taking him to some of the most remote locations across the globe—from the high Arctic to the Nubian desert. He has also written many original ideas for documentaries on diverse subjects—from asteroids to sharks—that have been commissioned by broadcasters worldwide. With his background in zoology and his lifelong interest in the great apes, he relished the chance to work on a feature film about chimpanzees. James also made the documentary *The Making of the Movie Chimpanzee*. His jungle flapjacks are legendary.

When not filming for *Chimpanzee*, Bill is a wildlife cameraman and research videographer at the Jane Goodall Institute. Initially, Bill, a former member of the US Peace Corps, spent just about every day following the wild chimpanzees of Gombe National Park in Tanzania, capturing the intimate details of their daily life. Film production companies have recognized Bill's talent and recruited him as a camera operator, videographer, and consultant for wildlife films shot at Gombe and in other parts of Africa. He has been a camera operator and scientific advisor for more than thirty productions, including the series *Chimp Week* and *Planet Earth*. Bill says that during his first fifteen years at Gombe, he spent more time with chimpanzees than with humans.

Born near London, Liz joined BBC White City in 1978 and worked in studio management before moving into production with music and arts documentaries. She relocated to Bristol in 1994 to work on a natural history series about the human animal, and for the past twelve years has been working in the independent sector. Although *Chimpanzee* is Liz's first feature film, she reckons there's nothing quite like the stark practicalities of listing, shifting, and safely delivering one and a half tons of film equipment across Africa.

Samuel Munene
Camera Assistant

Born in Kenya, Samuel is known for his incredible patience and accuracy in spotting wildlife miles away. Samuel's fitness, love of marathon walking, and wisdom made him the most valuable support to Bill in the forests of Uganda.

Before the team could set up and start shooting, there was the small matter of where they would stay for the three years it would take to film the movie. An existing camp in the Taï forest housed the Ivorian field assistants and two or three of Christophe's research students. There simply wasn't enough room for the film crew. The team would need sleeping quarters, a kitchen, electricity, and state-of-the-art technical facilities—in the middle of the jungle.

Ed Anderson, who formerly led biological expeditions to carry out wildlife surveys in remote regions, was hired as logistics manager. His task was to create a home in the rain forest from scratch within three months, before the torrential rains of the wet season arrived. Ed's main problem was the remoteness of the chimpanzees' territory. It was a two-day drive from the nearest major city, Abidjan, and an hour and a half from the nearest town, Taï, followed by a forty-five-minute walk through the rain forest. Everything would have to be carried in by hand—or rather, as Ed was to discover, by head.

In July 2008, Ed hired a team of Ivorian porters, who transported all the construction materials—as well as a gas cooker and a fridge—on their heads, making the grueling journey five or six times a day. As their boss, Ed wanted to show that he was strong enough—and not too proud or lazy—to do what he was asking the Ivorians to do . . . which is how he found himself that August balancing a sixty-six-pound plank of wood on his head, praying that it would not slip off, with tears in his eyes from the pain, drenched in sweat, all the while attempting to smile and joke with the porters.

Shortly after Ed arrived at camp, he had to go into Taï for supplies. By the time he'd finished his errands and was able to return to the forest, it was dark and pouring rain. As he negotiated the track through the jungle, he managed to get his Land Cruiser stuck in a huge puddle in the muddy, potholed track. "I decided to leave the vehicle there and run the rest of the way to camp," he says. As he was sprinting back, he saw a leopard on the path ahead of him. He skidded to a halt. The leopard paused, too. Ed's heart was in his mouth. The leopard was only a few yards away from him. Then the big cat slowly turned and disappeared into the darkness.

A little farther along the track, Ed found that the driving rain had made the river burst its banks and flood the trail, right at a junction in the track. Ed had no idea which way to go. It's easy to get lost in the jungle, even in good daylight conditions. As Ed stood in the dark, drenched by the driving rain, he remembered that only a few weeks ago a researcher in Congo had taken

OPPOSITE TOP: Laying out the foundations for the camp

OPPOSITE BOTTOM: The living and working quarters are almost finished.

the wrong path back to her camp. She had roamed around the forest for ten days before being found by poachers—the last people one would like to be rescued by. Ed waded on. Unable to see where he was putting his feet, he hoped that nothing in the cold water would bite him. He chose a path—and a few minutes later he realized, to his relief, it was the right one: up ahead was his makeshift camp.

Ed ended up driving the route between the town of Taï and the forest countless times during the construction of the camp—it was a five-hour round trip even for a box of nails or bag of sugar. Every journey ended with the Land Cruiser visiting the mechanics. During the first two months of construction, the porters carried into the rain forest—on their heads—two and a half tons of cement, seven tons of wood, four hundred sheets of roofing tin, four truckloads of sand, four truckloads of gravel, six water tanks, four beds and mattresses, three sinks, a toilet, a shower, and a stove, plus all the other equipment required to live in the forest for months at a time. "Without the strength, effort, and motivation of the Ivorian porters and builders," Ed affirms, "there is no way the camp would ever have been finished."

When it was completed, Ed's house had a concrete floor, wooden walls, a corrugated iron roof, and corrugated plastic for windows. It had double beds with mattresses in the bedrooms, a kitchen with a gas stove and a sink, a sitting room, and a toilet and shower block outside. There was even a dining room table. The sitting room would house all the camera equipment; the team had specially made "hot boxes" powered by a bank of car batteries. They would be used to heat the camera every night in order to drive the moisture out of it and help prevent mold growing inside the lenses.

"Ed did an amazing job," says Martyn Colbeck, the principal cameraman at Taï. "It was as civilized as it could be—in a forest." Martyn, a man who likes his wine, adds, "I insisted on decent wine glasses. These things make a big difference. Any fool can be uncomfortable."

OPPOSITE TOP: The interior of the finished camp

OPPOSITE BOTTOM: Ed (left) and Martyn prepare a meal.

WINNING THE CHIMPANZEES' TRUST

Wild animals are wary of humans, and scientists studying them must win their subjects' trust. This process, called "habituation," can take years. In Africa, people have long killed chimpanzees for meat or medicinal purposes, so the chimps are frightened even by the sound of a human. In some cases, the apes never relax enough to allow people to study them.

When Christophe first began his chimp project in 1979, the chimpanzees fled as soon as they saw him. During the first two months of being in the jungle, he didn't see a single chimp. It was a long, arduous, draining experience that was frequently boring and frustrating. It took twenty months of continuously following the chimps before Christophe and Hedwige noticed the first sign of progress: some chimps would look at them for a short while before running away. "You get glimpses, you see a shadow, and you have to try to put the pieces of the puzzle together," says Christophe. In the first two years, in fact, the researchers saw the chimpanzees a mere 1 percent of the whole time they spent searching for them.

At first, all the chimpanzees looked alike to Christophe: black shadows in the forest undergrowth. He knew how to distinguish males from females by their reproductive organs, but beyond that he had no idea how to tell one individual from another. Then one day, something happened that kept his motivation going: he heard the sound of pounding in the forest—it was the chimps using tools! Every time the chimps stopped

(Continued on page 33)

On February 1, 2009, director Mark Linfield and cameraman Martyn Colbeck flew to the Ivory Coast to meet Ed. They arrived in the country's largest city, Abidjan, a two-day drive from the Taï forest. Between them they had almost 900 pounds of equipment. They then had to pick up food—550 pounds—which had to last for three months in the forest. In an unstable, impoverished country, they were in a vulnerable position. "Anyone could have stopped us and stolen everything," reports Martyn. Fortunately, the crew had arranged for a car with diplomatic license plates, and they reached the camp without incident.

The challenging process of capturing the chimpanzees' daily lives was only just beginning, though. Christophe was understandably concerned about the chimpanzees (see "Thirty Years of Taï Chimps" sidebar). The chimps he studied were accustomed to a very small number of scientists carrying virtually nothing; Christophe is famous in primatology circles for winning the chimps' trust by following them, taking only a notebook, pen, and an orange for the entire day. The team would be hauling lots of equipment into the forest and pointing the camera, with its large lens, directly at the chimps. Christophe was also worried about contagion; because chimpanzees are so closely related to humans, it would be possible for any member of the team to pass a disease on to the apes. Finally, he was concerned about the crew's fitness: it is hard enough just walking ten to fifteen miles every day, let alone running after animals in a jungle while lugging heavy loads.

In order to break the crew in to the rigors ahead, Christophe devised what the film crew called a "chimp boot camp." Martyn recalls, "One of the big challenges for us was to work in a way that was practical to film but still meant that we were sensitive and respectful around the chimpanzees and didn't alarm them." Christophe wanted to re-create what it was like to follow chimpanzees before letting the crew near the animals. "We left camp with Christophe," Martyn continues, "and the first thing he did was walk very quickly through the most difficult, the most horrible, the densest forest that he could possibly find."

After half a mile, Christophe got down on all fours and pretended to be a chimpanzee. Martyn quickly realized that he was supposed to film Christophe. Ed was carrying the tripod so Martyn indicated where the tripod should go and at what height Ed should adjust it to, while Martyn swiftly got out his camera and set up the shot. Just as Martyn was sliding the camera onto the tripod, Christophe ran off. "He was deliberately trying to lose us!" exclaims Martyn.

ABOVE: Mark, Martyn, and Christophe are ready for boot camp.

The cameraman and Ed packed up their equipment as fast as possible and raced after Christophe. Mark hung back with the extra gear so that the chimps (played by Christophe) would not be alarmed by the numerous people following them—but if he stayed too far behind, he risked getting lost. "It all seemed a bit weird," says Martyn. "It was quite an amusing test to go through, with a scientist pretending to be a chimpanzee. But I realized that Christophe had to have faith in us; he needed to be convinced that we knew how to behave with the chimpanzees."

"It's extremely hard to explain to people how difficult it is to follow chimpanzees in the forest," Christophe relates, "so I thought this was the best way to make it understandable. Generally, I was pleased with how the team behaved and how sensitive Martyn was toward the chimpanzees." The crew had passed Christophe's test. Although the team joked and moaned about the "boot camp," in reality, their ordeal lasted only a day! Little did they realize how much more difficult it was going to be filming real chimpanzees for months at a stretch.

(Continued from page 32)

banging, Christophe would freeze; when they resumed, he was able to creep a little closer. He spotted a clearing in the jungle. As he approached, the chimps melted away into the trees.

When he entered the clearing, he saw that it was littered with coula nuts and shells. The chimpanzees had been using wooden branches as hammers to crack open the nuts—but they'd only left one wooden hammer. It was an enigma. How did all the chimps manage to crack nuts with just one hammer? Had they taken some hammers with them? Much later, Christophe discovered that when hammers are in short supply, the chimps may cooperate, with one individual cracking nuts and another fetching them in the hope that the hammer-owner will share.

Over the years, Christophe gradually drew closer to the chimps. Their nut cracking helped: the noise they made covered his approach, and if they were concentrating on their tool use, he was able to get nearer than usual. He found that many chimps would continue their work if he pretended not to be looking directly at them.

Over time, Christophe noticed that he could tell the chimps apart by distinguishing marks and coloration on their faces: some animals had scars, and some had faces that were darker or rounder than others. "After many years, I recognize them from the way they walk, the look in their eyes, and their voice," he says. "Salomé has a dancing walk and watery look; Héra, a serious expression and a cut on her left ear; Macho is round and totally black with a high-pitched voice; and Brutus has a gentle expression in spite of two deep cuts in the ears that give him a buccaneer appearance."

Part Two

Movies are incredibly expensive to make, so teams of writers typically spend months working on the script before the director and cameraman begin filming. In this case, the process was going to be much harder because no one knew what the "actors" would do—and they certainly couldn't be directed. Mark and Alastair had met up with Christophe at the Max Planck Institute prior to their first trip to the jungle in order to work out which chimps would be the best to concentrate on. They were looking for the most fascinating characters, the chimps with complex sets of relationships and friendships so that interesting events would happen to them—fingers crossed!—over the three-year filming period.

In that chrome and glass building, sitting around a table, the men came up with the bones of a script that would later be fleshed out by real events in Taï. Bill Wallauer, using his considerable knowledge of chimp behavior, made some suggestions, but Christophe suggested that the crew focus on a female he called Sumatra. She was comfortable being followed by Christophe and his students. She had a baby he called Sassandra and a confident little toddler, Shogun, who was a real "cock of the walk," as Mark put it. Even better, Sumatra had a large family and many friends. "Chimps are like humans— some are antisocial and some are well connected," notes Mark. "For the film, we wanted to choose chimpanzees who were at the center of everything."

But the situation in the jungle turned out to be rather different from the plans so carefully laid out in an air-conditioned office in Germany. The first filming trip, made by Bill, Ed, and Alastair, took place from September to November 2008. It was the wet season, and the team struggled with difficult conditions: torrential rain, low light levels, and a distinct coolness on the part of the leading lady, Sumatra, who seemed to dislike being filmed. One crucial part of the script was chimpanzee warfare. Like some human tribes, groups of chimpanzees will fight each other, sometimes with deadly consequences, as they attempt to expand their territories (see "War!" sidebar). But as the team discovered, although the Taï chimps do engage in territorial disputes, the thickness of the foliage and the darkness of the forest made these encounters almost impossible to film.

LEFT: Martyn has to wear a surgical mask while filming the chimps.

The directors and Bill decided that it would make more sense if Bill were to film the rival gang described in the script in another location: Ngogo in Kibale National Park, Uganda (see "Kibale National Park" sidebar). The Ngogo chimpanzees are infamous in primatology circles for engaging in frequent and often bloody battles. Filming them in more open forest would, everyone felt, be more practical—and far more dramatic.

It might sound unjustifiable to use chimpanzees in Uganda to play the parts of a group living in the Ivory Coast but, in Hollywood movies, it is commonplace to use actors when filming a true story and doesn't make the underlying story any less true. The directors felt there was nothing to be gained by showing the audiences pictures of a bush rustling in the darkness while the narrator described a fight no one would be able to see!

So the team packed up, and Bill, Kristin, Ed, and Mark flew to Ngogo in November 2008. Over the course of the three years it took to make the movie, Bill and Kristin returned to Ngogo five times (see "Filming the Rivals," Part III).

Meanwhile, back in the UK, cameraman Martyn was training hard to get fit enough to step into Bill's shoes and film in Taï. Martyn ran, cycled, and trekked for miles. A few days before filming, he was out running when he felt an excruciating pain in his lower leg. He assumed that he'd snapped his Achilles tendon—which would certainly have prevented him from filming. Fortunately, the injury was only a torn calf muscle. Even so, he needed substantial physical therapy to make sure he was well enough to leave on time.

Martyn did not have Bill's experience in filming chimpanzees, hence Christophe's insistence that he complete the chimp boot camp. Martyn passed with flying colors. But as Bill had felt, Martyn's biggest problem was that the star of the movie, Sumatra, simply wasn't interested in being filmed.

"The chimpanzees were making decisions about whether they would allow themselves to be filmed," recounts Martyn. "Maybe some of them felt uncomfortable having a camera lens pointed at them or about being the focus of our attention." As soon as Sumatra saw Martyn getting the camera out, she would simply turn her back or walk off. "I quickly realized that I was never going to be able to build a film around an individual that didn't want to be filmed," says Martyn. But everyone was at a loss when it came to choosing a replacement for the film's leading lady.

Another problem was the conditions. The Taï forest proved to be an even more physically arduous place to work than the team had imagined. The crew had to walk three miles to reach the chimps in the morning, follow them for six miles during the course of their daily activities, and walk the three miles back to camp at the end of the day. Martyn carried the thirty-seven-pound camera, and Ed had the sixty-six-pound tripod; Mark or one of the Ivorian assistants followed with food, spare batteries, and more camera equipment.

The forest was thick with vegetation and tangled with vines called lianas. "They're incredibly tough, like arrester wires, so it's so easy to trip because they don't break," says Martyn. "The worst thing is when they get you across the chest because they literally stop you in your tracks."

The film crew quickly learned the drill. They'd follow the chimpanzees until they stopped, then Martyn would indicate to Ed where to put the tripod while he got out the camera, just as they had done in boot camp. However, with real chimps, the pair had to be much faster. The tripod slowed them down as it is an ungainly, cumbersome piece of equipment; the forest floor is uneven and yet the tripod had to be perfectly level. The pair worked out that it was better to pack the equipment away properly each time the chimpanzees moved because carrying the camera and tripod over their shoulders slowed them down and meant they became ensnared in the lianas more often. "You never knew if the chimps were going to move a few yards or several miles," says Martyn. Ed would normally get left behind as he packed up the tripod, and he would have to try and catch up with the others, and the chimps, by listening for them or radioing the team.

Filming the chimps while behaving sensitively around them was, as Martyn had guessed during boot camp, a challenge. It took a lot of concentration to work out how to film the chimps through such thick jungle—and because of the risk of passing on diseases, Martyn had to stay at least seven yards from them. But the density of the vegetation meant the chimpanzees were nearly invisible if they were more than ten yards away, leaving a scant three-yard window from which to observe them! Moreover, staring directly at the chimpanzees made them uneasy. "I had to adopt this quite casual way of assessing a potential shot every time I stopped," recalls Martyn, "so I had to look away, look back at them, and then move position before deciding whether to film."

Christophe explained to Martyn that although chimpanzees are many times stronger than a grown man, human beings look threatening to them, and Martyn is a tall, broad-shouldered guy. By turning sideways, Martyn was able to make himself look smaller and less alarming. "But it still took the chimps quite a while to get used to the number of people and the amount of equipment," says Martyn.

Making his task even more difficult was the low light level that had concerned Mark so much on the recce. On cloudy days it was frequently too dark to film anything, whereas on sunny days the contrast between the black chimpanzees in the shadows and the bright patches of vegetation was simply too great; the camera rendered the shadows as solid black, with no detail, and the lighter spots as solid white.

"I found that the perfect light to film in was hazy but bright," notes Martyn. But even bright overcast days could be dark on the forest floor, and the situation was made worse by having a black subject that absorbed what little light there was. This led to some difficult decisions about camera equipment.

Normally, movies made in such low light conditions would be shot with "prime" lenses as these create sharp images at wide apertures (when the lens is wide open to take in as much light as possible). But while prime lenses excel at taking in light, the view offered by each lens is fixed, whereas a zoom lens can give a wide-angle view and then be rapidly zoomed in to produce a close-up of a chimp's face without the need to change lenses. Martyn opted for a zoom because the opportunities to film chimpanzee behavior were so few and far between that he couldn't afford to risk missing shots as he changed lenses. This compromised the image quality but maximized the chances of capturing great footage. And because a single zoom lens can do the job of five prime lenses, each of which is optimized for a different distance, it was a popular choice with the porters, too!

Regardless of the lens Martyn used, the low light levels required the lens to be set at a wide aperture, which in turn forced Martyn to deal with a shallow depth of field. In other words, the section of picture that appeared in focus was extremely narrow. Frequently if one eye of a chimpanzee was sharp, the other eye would appear out of focus! On a big screen, these differences are noticeable and can be a real problem. It's little wonder that one of the Ivorian assistants, Arsene Sioblo, commented, "Martyn is never happy."

Nut Cracking

*A*fter a first filming trip that was fraught with difficult conditions and evasive subjects, the crew was frustrated. But seven months later, they returned to the Ivory Coast, and the team's fortunes finally changed. One day in March 2009, the filmmakers were trekking through the forest when they heard noises echoing through the trees. *Tock, tock, tock . . . crack!* The team followed the noise and emerged into a clearing fringed by evergreen coula trees. There were chimpanzees everywhere! Some members of the south group were sitting peacefully, the adults involved in the serious business of cracking open the walnutlike coula nuts while the youngsters played or begged for the shelled nuts. It was the perfect scene—just what the crew had been waiting for.

The team watched as each of the adults gathered up a handful of nuts and placed them dexterously in faint depressions in the tree roots (known as "anvils") before tapping the nuts with a "hammer"—a wooden branch (see "The Tool Users of Taï" sidebar for a more detailed explanation of these hammers and anvils). Some of the chimps used one hand to grasp short, stout hammers; others held long, thin branches with a hand at either end.

"Of all the things that the chimps do in Taï forest, I think this is the most fascinating and intriguing behavior to watch," says Martyn. "The chimps look so human." Christophe has excavated some buried hammers and carbon-dated the soil around them. The soil—and presumably the hammers—dates back 4,000 years, so for at least that time chimpanzees have been returning to the same spots in the forest and using the same types of hammers.

The chimps would often stay for hours in these clearings, sometimes returning two or three times during the day. That allowed the crew to rest and film entire sequences in good light. Even more important, the team had time to learn to recognize individuals. It was here that they first became aware of the dynamics taking place within this group of chimpanzees.

The hammers are always left behind in the clearings where the chimpanzees go to crack nuts, and because chimpanzees are so hierarchical, the dominant individuals get their pick of sitting places, hammers, and anvils. On one occasion, the team watched as low-ranking Julia begged to use the hammer that high-ranking Sumatra was wielding. Sumatra completely ignored Julia, even when Julia leaned in so that she was barely inches from Sumatra's face.

Another time, Martyn watched as alpha male Freddy was cracking panda nuts and Athos wanted to borrow his hammer. Panda nuts are much harder than coula nuts, and the chimps have to use stones as hammers to extract

the kernel. When Freddy wandered off to fetch some more nuts, leaving his hammer behind, Athos looked over his shoulder to check that Freddy wasn't looking, picked up Freddy's stone, and ran off with it. When Freddy returned with his nuts, he looked around and couldn't find his tool. He tried to use a wooden hammer, but it snapped. He picked another one; it wasn't up to the task. His third hammer broke in two. He threw the end away. "The expression on his face was one of total disgust and annoyance," affirms Martyn.

In sharp contrast to this competitive behavior was the nurturing attitude shown by mothers toward their offspring. The crew noticed that the mothers shared nuts with their babies and patiently taught their older offspring how to crack nuts on their own. The learning process can take years, as evidenced by the sheer frustration on the faces of the little ones as they pound and pound a nut that refuses to crack.

OPPOSITE and TOP: A young chimp learns how to crack open a coula nut.

THE TOOL USERS OF TAI

As the coula nuts ripen, the chimpanzees grab wooden hammers—short, stout branches—and then climb into the trees. They crack the small, hard nuts directly against large branches with their hammers. The whole forest vibrates with the noise of the apes bashing nuts. Christophe says, "When ten to fifteen females and youngsters are pounding in the trees around you for hours at a time, it sounds as if a team of carpenters is at work."

Once the nuts fall from the trees, the chimps collect as many as fifteen at a time and carry them to a large root, which they use as an anvil. The fallen branches they employ as hammers naturally come in many different shapes, sizes, weights, and degrees of hardness; the chimps' skill is in selecting a branch (or even a small stone) that allows them to crack a nut open within six hits and eat over two nuts a minute. Each nut is 50 percent fat; the best nut crackers consume up to 270 nuts each day, netting them over 3,000 calories—one and a half times as many calories as a human female needs daily.

Many of the female chimps aren't able to eat all their nuts, though. When they're about a year old, youngsters will start to beg for nuts from their mothers. Most mothers are generous and give away about 40 percent of their nuts. When he began his research, Christophe was particularly interested in learning whether chimpanzees teach their infants, and in nut cracking, he saw a unique opportunity to observe whether chimps share this trait with humans.

He noticed that when Sumatra's son Shogun was five years old, she started to give him opportunities to crack nuts himself. For instance, she'd go off to search for more nuts but leave intact nuts and a hammer behind, pointedly putting them next to the anvil. On other occasions, Christophe observed that Sumatra wouldn't leave a hammer, but would instead place a whole nut on the anvil ready to be pounded. On these occasions, Shogun would still pick up an ineffective hammer so sometimes Sumatra ended up sharing hers with him.

It shows how much time and effort chimpanzees put into helping their offspring develop—again, a very human characteristic—for not only do chimpanzee mothers share their nuts with their young for years, they also spend years imparting the skill to their offspring. Shogun had learned how to crack coula nuts by the time Sumatra gave birth to his younger sister, but it took him four more years to master the art of cracking the extremely hard panda nuts, which can only be opened with heavy stone hammers. Sumatra continued both sharing panda nuts with Shogun and providing him with good hammers and intact nuts for practice until he was eight years old! It's not uncommon to see mothers caring for two youngsters at the same time, breastfeeding the youngest and sharing nuts with both of them, while making sure the older one has access to good nuts and tools.

Cracking nuts with a hammer seems so human. When watching young chimpanzees as they struggled to learn this new skill, Christophe always felt like making suggestions: "Don't you see the hammer is touching the ground in front of the nut? Change your grip on the hammer! Place the nut in a shallow hole! Hold the nut to stop it falling off the anvil!" To test whether he had actually judged the problems correctly, he tried cracking nuts himself.

"To my dismay," he says, "I have to admit that even after years of practice, I was unable to come close to Sumatra's performance. Sumatra used the exact force needed to just crack the shell and could therefore extract the nut fully intact. To my embarrassment, I would regularly use too much force and smash the nut. I would then have to spend ages trying to sort the edible parts from the smashed pieces of shell. I gained a lot of respect for these chimpanzees, who are able to crack two nuts a minute for hours on end."

Watching the chimpanzees crack nuts was the perfect way to work out who the new cast of the film should be. "People often find it very difficult to tell the difference between individual animals of the same species, but what struck me, seeing the chimpanzees in that clearing for the first time, was just how individual they all were," recounts Martyn. "It's like going into a bar full of people; everyone looks different."

For practicality's sake, it was decided that the new characters would be the chimpanzees that didn't mind being filmed (see "Chimp Favorites" sidebar). And as the crew got to know the new cast, the chimpanzees' personalities revealed themselves in all their complexities. Mark recalls that when the team first arrived, they would sit around the dinner table at night looking bewildered as the researchers described, in great detail, differences in the chimps' characters. "If you walked in and hadn't realized what we were talking about, you'd be forgiven for thinking we were discussing friends or a TV soap opera," he says.

Comments such as "He is always behaving like that when his mother is around. He starts fights and expects her to come to his rescue, but one day he'll pay for it, powerful mother or not!" were not uncommon. Not only were the researchers able to identify each individual by subtle differences in body hair or face shape, they knew the chimpanzees' personalities and relationships intimately. Soon the film crew too was gossiping around the dinner table about the chimps.

The chimpanzees are often given strange and exotic-sounding names, such as Kuba or Zyon. Chimp babies tend to be named by either the researcher or the field assistants who were following the mother when she was pregnant. The general rule is that babies will be given a name starting with the same letter as their mother, but after that it's up to individual taste!

BIENVENUE
Female, estimated age 17
Mother of Balou

CARAMEL
Male, age 9

BALOU
Female, age 2

JULIA
Female, estimated age 41

COCO
Female, age 21
Mother of Caramel

ZYON
Male, estimated age 47
Father of Kuba and Ibrahim

KUBA
Male, age 15

OLIVIA
Female, estimated age 38

SUMATRA
Female, estimated age 46
Mother of Sagu, Shogun, and Sassandra

IBRAHIM
Male, age 11

ROMARIO
Male, age 12
Older brother of Ravel

SAGU
Male, age 22

KINSHASA
Female, age 21
Older sister of Kuba

RAVEL
Male, age 8
Younger brother of Romario

SHOGUN
Male, age 10

SASSANDRA
Female, age 4

WAPI
Female, estimated age 43
Mother of Woodstock and Wala

LOUISE
Female, age 31
Mother of Lilou

TABOO
Male, age 19

WOODSTOCK
Male, age 17

LILOU
Male, age 4

UTAN
Male, age 17

WALA
Female, age 6

PINCER
Male, age 38

MWEYA
Male, age 42

SCAR
Male, age 37

*A*fter the crew had spent several days filming the chimps nut cracking, they were lucky enough to see the chimpanzees hunting. The team realized something was happening when the chimps went into stealth mode, silently disappearing into the forest canopy. In contrast, the red colobus monkeys the chimps were hunting were terrified, their cries earsplitting as they attempted to escape.

Chimpanzees are simply too heavy to pursue the more agile colobus monkeys into the fragile branches of the treetops, so they get around the problem by cooperating: some males will block a monkey's escape route while others herd it toward waiting hunters (see "Catching Monkeys" sidebar). It was extremely exciting, but the fast action proved frustrating to film. "All you're getting, at any one point, is a glimpse of one chimp suddenly moving, passing through an open clearing, and jumping into the next tree," says Martyn.

The crew found it difficult to follow the chimps' progress through the trees, as they would disappear and then reappear in unpredictable places. When they did appear, the chimps were visible only as black shapes in the canopy, silhouetted against the sky. On the ground, the Ivorian assistants tried to help by pointing to where they thought the hunters were heading. Martyn abandoned the tripod and held the camera on his shoulder as he desperately tried to track the chimps.

Several of the monkeys huddled together in a wild mango tree, so Martyn decided to film them, hoping the chimps would come to their prey. As Martyn stood below, two of the hunters burst upon the mango tree and reached to grab a monkey—which fell from the branches, plummeting toward Martyn and landing on his shoulder! Dazed, the colobus tumbled to the ground. Martyn swung around, but at that moment, one of the male chimpanzees, Kuba, leaped down and grabbed the monkey. He paused and glanced at Martyn as if to make sure the cameraman wasn't going after the monkey, too, and then disappeared into the forest with his prize.

The chimpanzees' silence was broken. The forest erupted into screams of excitement as the hunters converged on Kuba and the monkey and the rest of the chimp group raced to catch up with them. Martyn, annoyed that he'd missed the shot of Kuba catching the colobus, ran in the direction of the noise. He and the rest of the team stumbled onto a scene of complete chaos. The group was gathered around a giant mahogany tree, the males beating the huge supporting roots of nearby trees and screaming, the females shrieking and holding out their hands, begging for meat. In the center of the group,

OPPOSITE: Male chimps about to close in on their prey

two males were tearing the colobus apart. "Everyone was trying to get a piece of meat," recalls Martyn. "It was absolute bedlam—a massive amount of screaming and some actual fighting." Once the still-warm flesh had been divided up, the chimps settled down to quietly eat their kill (see "Catching Monkeys" sidebar for details on how the chimps divide the meat).

A hunt was exactly the kind of dramatic sequence that the movie needed, and fortunately the crew was able to capture a number of hunts over their three years in the forest.

CATCHING MONKEYS

Hunting cooperatively is yet another example of a skill at which chimpanzees excel. All chimpanzee populations hunt, and usually their prey are monkeys. In the Taï forest, the chimpanzees chase mostly colobus monkeys.

The only way that chimpanzees can hope to catch the lighter and more agile monkeys is to cooperate. This complex behavior is rarely seen in the animal kingdom, apart from a handful of other social species, such as wolves and dolphins. The chimps hunt in pairs or groups of up to ten males (Taï groups average four or five members), who coordinate their actions with each other. Hunters must be flexible, fast, and able to quickly grasp what other team members are doing—and they must anticipate what the prey's next move might be.

A team of two finds it hard to outwit and outstrip a monkey, and only every fifth hunt is successful. Groups of more than four hunters, however, will catch a monkey two out of three tries. It takes a long time to learn how to hunt efficiently; youngsters can't learn from their mothers since females don't hunt so young males tend to team up with older males who'll act as role models.

Youngsters start learning to hunt when they're around six years old, but they won't become skilled until they are thirty.

Although all chimpanzees hunt, in Taï the chimps are unusually cooperative. Male red colobus monkeys can be aggressive, but the chimpanzees' desire for meat overrides their fear of being attacked. The male chimps hunt every third day and eat, on average, half a pound of meat daily.

In a typical hunt, young, inexperienced chimps like Taboo flush the prey out while more experienced males like Zyon try to block the monkey's escape route. The "driver" chimps push the prey toward the ambushers, who close in on the monkey.

Only one chimpanzee catches and kills the monkey, but other members of the hunt quickly join the victor, screaming and displaying excitement. The atmosphere can feel like that of a World Cup soccer game. The meat is shared with the other hunters as well as with the rest of the group, who rush to join the victors. The resulting scene may look chaotic, with every chimp trying to grab some meat, but Christophe's observations of hundreds of hunts reveal that strict meat-sharing rules are enforced.

Hunters receive more meat than nonhunters; the chimps whose decisive actions led directly to the capture of the monkey get the most. Females, since they don't hunt, often end up with little or nothing. But since chimpanzee society is intensely hierarchical, a few dominant females may end up with almost as much meat as some males. A large monkey, weighing around twenty pounds, might be shared among a group of twenty chimps. It usually takes about two hours for the monkey to be divided up and eaten.

TOP: One of the hunters howls in excitement.

RIGHT: A bristled male chimpanzee rushes in to claim his share of a captured monkey.

THE ANIMALS OF THE FOREST YOU NEVER SEE

The Taï forest has an incredible diversity of wildlife—but the crew saw few animals because many of the creatures there are extremely shy of people. Some of the forest's rarer animals are nocturnal or crepuscular (they venture out at dusk), such as the leopard (next page), the pygmy hippo (top right), and our largest land mammal, the African elephant (top left). These hard-to-spot animals were captured using a remote camera triggered by the interruption of an infrared beam. Although red river hogs are normally active at night too, these hogs (opposite) were shot during the day, allowing us to see their beautiful markings. Mangabeys, a ground-dwelling monkey (bottom left, front), are relatively common in Taï, but a number of species of tiny antelope, called forest duikers, are unique to Taï. This one (bottom left, back) was caught loitering behind the mangabey. Other "models" caught on film were a flock of White-breasted Guineafowl (bottom right).

LEOPARD ATTACKS

In September 1987, attracted by chimpanzee and monkey alarm calls, Christophe found the first chimp he ever followed, Falstaff, covered in blood. Falstaff had sixteen wounds, all inflicted by a leopard. Leopards are the main natural predators that chimpanzees have to fear in the Taï forest; they are supreme ambush hunters, armed with ferocious claws and teeth. Falstaff's wounds healed rapidly except for one neat little hole in his side, from which a whitish secretion continually oozed. His health deteriorated until he was no longer strong enough to follow the group. He died two months after the attack.

Christophe believes that the threat of leopards has caused the Taï chimps to alter their behavior in comparison with chimpanzees in other parts of Africa. Partly this is because the likelihood of a leopard attack may be much higher for Taï chimps than for other populations: there are ten times as many leopards in the Taï forest as there are in less dense rain forests. In a five-year period, an average of seventeen Taï chimps are injured by leopards. Perhaps because of this threat, Taï chimpanzees—both males and females—will often try to rescue group members under attack by a leopard—a behavior not often witnessed with other chimpanzee populations.

OPPOSITE: A leopard captured with a remotely operated camera

Christophe was in the forest with the chimpanzees when he heard the painful-sounding cries of a female. The chimp mothers he was following started barking their loud *waa waa* alarm cries and rushed in the direction of the female's screams. Christophe ran after them, although he didn't know what was happening. As he reached the besieged female, he saw four adult chimps hurtling at high speed toward a leopard. The leopard had attacked the female, but on seeing the group arrive, it turned and fled.

Even more extraordinary was the sight of chimpanzees using weapons to fight off a leopard. Christophe first saw this in 1989. Seven chimpanzees chased a leopard, which hid in a hole under a fallen tree. The chimpanzees picked up fallen branches and tried to beat the big cat with them, sometimes stabbing it with the ends of their sticks.

Not only will chimps come to the rescue of other members of their group, but everyone is extremely solicitous of leopard victims, regularly licking wounds and removing dirt. This helps wounds heal more rapidly, particularly ones the injured chimp can't reach. After years of observation, Christophe believes that leopard attacks have made these apes, particularly females, more social and supportive than other populations of chimpanzees throughout Africa.

*S*ound is an aspect of a film that the audience is often barely aware of, yet it's key to creating an enjoyable and immersive movie. "Sound works in a totally different way in the cinema than it does on television," comments Mark. "You have proper surround sound, so you can almost transport people to the rain forest." It was critical to get a good sound track, so over the course of the three years she spent in the forest, Kristin Mosher set out to capture the wide range of sounds the chimps make to communicate with each other.

Because chimps are so social and highly excitable, there were many sounds to record. But at the same time, their variable behavior can present quite the task for a sound recordist. In a split second, they can go from silent to shouting so loudly it hurts your ears—and ruins the recording! "Most times there are signs that quiet chimps are about to become wildly boisterous," Kristin notes. "The challenge is to predict what's going to happen and who is about to vocalize so that I can alter my recording levels accordingly. For instance, if I'm with a group of chimps that are resting quietly and they hear other chimps call in the distance, there is a good chance they will respond with their own calls." She says that her favorite chimp sound is their laughter. It's very soft, so the recording levels need to be set high to ensure that it's audible on a sound track.

Recording the chimps' calls was essential for the film sound track, but in order to really immerse the audience into the chimps' forest home, the rich variety of sounds of the forest had to be captured as well. And when Ed wasn't racing through the forest after Martyn, shouldering the tripod, he was tasked with recording atmospheric jungle noises. As Ed says, "After a day in the jungle, all the trees and vines start to look the same: an impenetrable mass of green. But the sound of the forest is one thing that changes constantly."

On one perfect day in May 2010, Ed and Martyn followed the chimps to a clearing in the forest created by a fallen tree. It was mid-afternoon, and most of the adult chimps were lying along the length of the fallen tree's trunk, resting in the heat after a morning of fig eating, while the youngsters played and skipped around. The sky—what could be seen of it through the dense foliage—was a brilliant clear blue. Shafts of sunlight filtered through the leaves. Although the chimps, for once, were being extremely quiet, Ed kept the microphone on and picked up the sounds of the forest: the wind in the trees; tinkerbirds, whose *tink tink* calls sound like hammers hitting metal; the occasional chimp scratch; a tree branch breaking; cicadas; flies and bees buzzing. In the distance, a group of black colobus monkeys was feeding in

the trees, their calls a bellowing chorus that sounded like a suitcase being dragged across gravel. A hornbill flew by, laughing wheezily.

This idyllic scene was shattered by a mischievous adolescent male chimp, Ibrahim, who spotted a group of mangabeys, ground-dwelling monkeys that live in large groups of up to a hundred. He grabbed the trunk of a sapling, shook it at them, and stamped his feet. The mangabey group erupted with hysterical shrieks and fled. Ibrahim careered after them, banging on tree roots in his excitement.

The banes of sound recordists in the Western world are planes flying by at inopportune moments. "Even in the middle of the jungle," Ed observes, "there are noises that can make recording the simplest of sounds problematic. Branches swaying as the chimps travel through the trees sound more like white noise than leaves. Flies attracted to the fake fur of the microphone wind-cover buzz distractingly around it at exactly the wrong moment. Cicadas take turns calling to one another, the racket so loud it drowns out the more subtle sounds of the forest.

"But despite all the obstacles, the times when we were sitting in the forest, completely enveloped in sound, and managed to record those multiple layers, or finally capture one of the calls that had long eluded us—like the resonant warble of the African grey parrot—made it all worthwhile," says Ed.

"I guess it's because it's so challenging that it's so enjoyable," agrees Kristin. "It's so rewarding when you've spent all day having quiet chimp vocalizations drowned out by the sounds of the forest and finally it's as if someone turns the volume down and it's perfectly quiet and I can record the little sounds of chimp laughter as they discover another tasty fruit tree."

LEFT: A male chimpanzee gives a "pant hoot" call.

——— A DAY IN THE FOREST ———

6 AM: Early morning sunlight filters through the milky plastic windows in the roof of the team's quarters. Fruit dislodged by the wind or spot-nosed monkeys hits the corrugated iron with a thud, waking the crew. The sounds of the forest grow—the hum of cicadas and the metallic clunks and clicks of hammer-headed fruit bats nesting in branches above the house.

Martyn is up first. (It's still the middle of the night as far as Ed and James are concerned.) He puts a kettle of water on to boil and heads off for a shower, muttering complaints under his breath because, in the high humidity of the forest, his towel never dries. The refreshingly cold shower is fed from tanks on the roof, which are filled with well water by Ivorian Petit Alain. James and Ed continue to sleep, choosing precious extra minutes in bed over a shower.

The crew members wear long underwear to protect their thighs from abrasions caused by walking long distances in the hot weather; they also wear two pairs of socks to prevent blisters. Martyn makes tea and has muesli with powdered milk (Martyn, ever prepared, brought muesli, tea, and chocolate bars with him from England).

James and Ed finally stir and wolf down some of last night's dinner. After

breakfast, Martyn and Ed prepare the equipment, taking the camera and lens out of their heated boxes and packing the camera, the ponchos, and a couple of one-liter water bottles into a rucksack. A walkie-talkie, spare battery, insect repellent, a notebook and pen, a head net in case of a bee attack, some flapjacks—freshly burned by James—and a Tupperware container with noodles and sardines for lunch are squeezed into a pocket of the rucksack. The guys wear long green trousers and shirts; the trousers hold the rest of the equipment: a compass, a GPS unit, lens cloths, surgical face masks, and a map showing the chimpanzees' territory.

Into another backpack go two Zeiss lenses, spare camera batteries, a pouch containing antihistamines and adrenalin in case of a serious bee attack, toilet paper, trash bags, and more face masks. This pack will be carried by one of the Ivorian assistants.

7:30 AM: The crew leaves camp. James sees them off and sits down at the field laptop in camp to log the previous day's rushes. The crew walks south past the researchers' house and the Ivorian field assistants' camp to the boot area. This is a covered spot where all the forest boots are kept. The team exchanges their sandals for rubber boots, then wash them in fresh water, followed by

chlorinated water to sterilize them. This helps prevent the transport of bacteria into the forest that could harm the chimps; crew members also wash their hands with chlorinated soap. As for the boots, although they are not comfortable over long-distance walks, they keep feet dry. Wearing hiking boots in such damp conditions could result in foot rot.

The field assistants have given the team the GPS coordinates of where the chimps spent the night. The chimps' sleeping places can be up to three miles away from the camp. As the crew gets closer to the location, the assistants, who have been following the chimps since dawn, radio back with updated positions. Once near the chimps, the team leaves the trail and heads straight into the jungle, trying to avoid being tripped up by lianas, stung by ants, or bitten by venomous snakes.

8:30 AM: The team can now hear the chimps. The males are drumming on hollow tree buttresses, large roots that come out of the trunk; one ape has picked a fight, and a noisy squabble breaks out. As the men draw closer, they give a specific signal to let the chimpanzees know that it's them and not strangers—like poachers—who pose a threat.

The film crew now puts on surgical face masks. The masks make it hard for crew members to breathe, particularly when they have to run to keep up with the chimps, and the masks quickly grow saturated with moisture from their breath. As a result, masks are changed three to four times a day. Wearing them helps prevent the chimps from catching human diseases to which they have no immunity.

The team can only rest when the chimps are resting, when there is nothing interesting to film, or when the light is too poor. If the chimps are moving or the light is good, they must press on, which means they may go for hours without eating.

No interaction with the chimpanzees is allowed, nor can anyone eat in front of them lest the chimps associate humans with food. When they get a chance, the filmmakers must slip away to eat their lunch out of sight of the chimps.

Usually the chimps travel six miles per day, feeding on fruit, resting, grooming, playing, and fighting as they go. If the team is lucky, it will be able to film tool use, hunting, and warfare.

4 PM: Martyn or Ed, plus a field assistant, follow the chimps until the light fades, and then the film crew hikes the three miles back to camp. An Ivorian assistant remains with the chimps to mark where they will spend the night (see "The Ivorian Field Assistants" sidebar).

5 PM: Back in the camp, it's time for tea and a bite to eat—cheese or chorizo and crackers. Martyn checks his equipment and what he has filmed and packs the camera and lenses away in the heated boxes. James downloads the footage and assesses the day's takings. He is often joined by the rest of the team, the researchers, and the Ivorians, all of whom are keen to see the result of their grueling fifteen-mile walk through the forest. Everyone relaxes for an hour: Martyn listens to podcasts or audiobooks, Ed plays the guitar or updates his diary, and James gets another French lesson from Petit Alain.

8 PM: James and Petit Alain cook—pasta or rice with sauce and chicken or chorizo sausage, perhaps, or one of

Petit Alain's fiery chilis. The crew has a gas-powered fridge and buys fresh vegetables and meat from the town of Taï every few days. The meal is usually followed by a glass or two of French wine and a petty argument.

10 PM: Everyone retires to bed. Ed lies awake, listening to the hammer-headed fruit bats. He says, "Their call sounds like hitting the end of an empty plastic tube with the palm of your hand, trying to make a musical beat: *tonk! tonk! tonk!*" Just as most of the team falls asleep, a tree hyrax emits an ear-piercing scream. Martyn snores loudly and drowns out another film James is trying to watch.

— THE IVORIAN FIELD ASSISTANTS —

One reason the Taï chimpanzee project has been so successful for three decades is Christophe's involvement of the local people. The Ivorian field assistants are crucial—their presence deters poachers, and, like the scientists, they observe the apes and collect data. With their help, Christophe has been able to collate information on multiple chimpanzee groups throughout the year, building up a picture of the chimpanzees, their behavior, and their relationships. At first, the villagers were wary of the apes, but through the assistants' knowledge of the jungle and the chimps, their attitude has become much more positive. "These men are our ambassadors for the forest," proclaims Christophe.

The field assistants follow the chimpanzees from the time the apes wake to when they sleep. The chimpanzees make nests in the canopy at night. The assistants then have an hour-long walk back to their camp. The chimps rise at 6 AM and the assistants need to be back at the chimps' nests before they get up in the morning as otherwise the group would disappear into the forest and be difficult to trace. This means the assistants have to rise around 4:30 AM and head into the jungle before 5 AM. From when it is light until it grows dark, the assistants collect data. And unlike the film crew, which works four days and then has a rest day, assistants work six days before getting a break.

ABOVE (clockwise from top left): Arsene Sioblo, Valentine Yagnon, Petit Alain Toubate, Alphonse Tagnon, Jean-Claude Blaihyo, and Charlie Hubert Biorou

By the end of the second filming trip, the team had shot some fantastic material—nut cracking and hunting—and they'd met the chimps who would be the key characters in the movie, the ones whose lives were unfolding in front of their lenses. They were also living in a mysterious and magical world, with both rare animals unique to Taï, such as the olive colobus, as well as marginally more common, but nonetheless wonderfully named, birds and beasts, like the copper-tailed glossy starling and Lord Derby's flying squirrel. A walk through the forest was always full of surprises, as Christophe discovered.

One day he was following the chimpanzees along a ridge when he heard loud alarm calls. "What immediately surprised me," he remembers, "was that these cries sounded anguished." As he approached, he saw the caller: a female chimp. She was high in a tree and calling incessantly, as if she needed help, yet she was surrounded by other chimpanzees. Christophe circled the tree, trying to spot the source of the chimp's distress, when he saw an adult leopard just thirty yards from the female. The big cat was twenty yards up in a tree. "I hadn't realized that leopards could climb that high," says Christophe.

The leopard was unaware of Christophe, who watched as the female chimpanzee the leopard had been stalking silently disappeared into the canopy. Then the leopard looked down, straight at Christophe. A moment later, she lunged at a tree trunk eight yards below her perch, dropped to the forest floor, and slipped into the jungle. Christophe stood still for five minutes, letting his heartbeat return to normal and the adrenaline pumping through his body to dissipate.

The rain forest is indeed full of surprises; some were as majestic as the leopard, but, as the crew found out, others were rather more unwelcome. In March 2009, Martyn and Ed were following the chimps on a particularly long march through the forest. Each was carrying over forty pounds of gear, and the heat and humidity were, as usual, sapping their energy. The chimps didn't show any signs of fatigue; the adults explored the trees while the young ones played games with each other and got up to all kinds of mischief. Suddenly, the chimps let out a communal shriek and ran off at a great pace. Martyn and Ed scrambled after them, not knowing what the plan was. It was then that they both heard buzzing around their ears, followed by a series of sharp, burning stings on their heads, necks, and arms.

The cheeky adolescent Ibrahim had disturbed a bees nest. The other chimps had sensed the bees, screamed, and scampered, leaving the insects to vent their anger on Ed and Martyn. The men picked up their packs and

ran as fast as they could. Ed had a bee right next to his ear, desperately attempting to sting him, as he ran and tried to swat it. By the time they'd shaken off the bees, Martyn's head and neck were covered in swollen hives. The following season, the two of them would be attacked by hornets.

During the wet season that year, between August and November, Ed and Martyn filmed the chimps fishing for ants—another example of tool use. The chimps break off sticks to a satisfactory length, sharpen an end, and poke the stick into an ant nest. As the ants attack the sticks, the chimps quickly pull the sticks out and suck off the ants before they can nip. The crew managed to capture the ant-fishing chimps on film, but failed to avoid the ants' vicious bites. "When we were steadying the camera or holding foliage out of the way of the lens we had to keep dead still," says Ed, "even though ants were crawling up our legs or down our arms."

Contending with biting insects in the jungle was bad enough, but unwelcome camp visitors proved to be even worse. One night, a venomous rhinoceros viper slithered into the sitting room, rested momentarily, and then headed straight for a bedroom. The team hit the ground around the snake with broom handles, hoping it would feel the vibrations and leave. Unsurprisingly, the frantic activity merely angered the snake—it coiled its body into a striking position. The team had no idea what to do. "We had a lengthy standoff. The snake was poised ready to strike, we were poised ready to run," recounts James. Finally the viper retreated across the concrete floor and out into the bush.

Another night James woke at 3 AM to find his mosquito net black with ants. He turned on his flashlight to discover his bed was swarming with them. These were the same driver ants the team had filmed in the rain forest, and now, like a marauding army, they were on the march. Driver ants march single file before suddenly spreading across the forest floor, wreaking havoc, killing, and eating everything in their path.

It was the middle of the night, and millions of ants had arrived, crawling all over the walls, the floors, and every pot and pan in the kitchen. Everyone ran to a patch of ground not covered in ants to brush them from their hair and clothes and think of a plan. Because ants' primary sense is smell (sensed not with a nose but with antennae), the team decided to pour generator fuel around the camp to create a foul-smelling barrier. It worked; ants still marching from the jungle turned back. But the crew still faced the lengthy task of getting rid of every biting ant from inside the camp . . .

Far more disgusting than the ants, though, were mango flies—a nuisance throughout this part of Africa. The flies laid their eggs on the team's clothes. The larvae are minute when they hatch, but use sharp "teeth" to bite their way beneath the skin, where they grow, feeding on human tissue. "The first

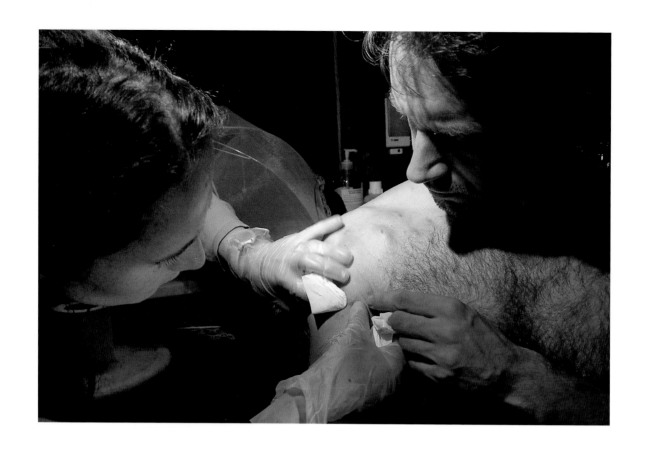

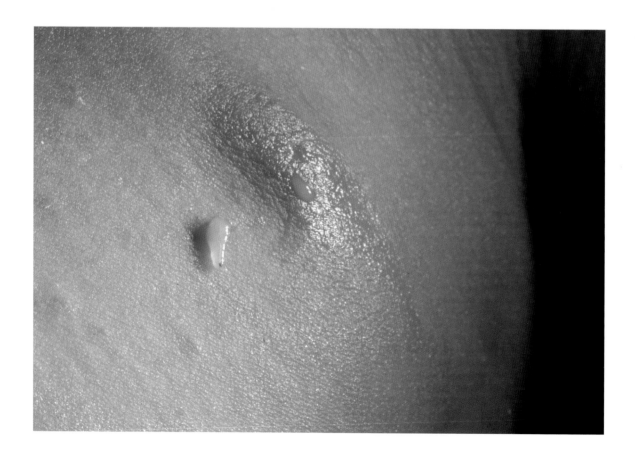

you know about them is you have an itchy bite," says James, "but within a couple of days, the area becomes swollen and sore and the itchiness is intermittently replaced with a grinding pain." The pain is caused by the maggot waking up for a meal.

At this stage, the maggot is too small to be squeezed out—there is a risk of killing it and leaving it to rot inside the body. "You have to grow it, feeding it your blood and flesh, until it's plump," specifies James. Covering the maggot's breathing hole with Vaseline suffocates the creature and it can then be squeezed out. The trauma and allergic reaction caused by having a maggot living and feeding on their flesh meant that the crew often had hard sores on their bodies months after the maggots had been removed. Altogether, the team usually had fifty maggots among them every season. At one point, Ed had twenty-seven on his shoulder, and Martyn had one on a rather more sensitive bit of his anatomy.

Even worse than the physical discomfort was the mental toll. By October 2009, Martyn had spent a total of six months in the forest—albeit not all at once—and had eight more left, spread across a three-year filming period. The cameraman was at his lowest point. He wrote in his diary, *I sometimes wonder if and how I can get to the end of this. Filming chimps in Taï is testing my patience and perseverance to the very limit. I am so constrained; I feel so boxed in. I am shooting a jigsaw of still images: vignettes through tiny windows in the dense forest.*

Martyn, as a photographer and cinematographer, felt he had few creative opportunities. The environment and the chimpanzees did not allow the kind of camera moves or breadth of equipment or even landscape shots that a film's director of photography would normally have to play with. He couldn't even film a sunset or a sunrise. He wrote, *I often look at the small patches of sky between the canopy and think about being somewhere else. Anywhere other than in this green prison where frustration is the order of each and every day.*

In spite of the difficulties of working in the rain forest, one aspect of the jungle that everyone, from the students to the crew, adored was the chimpanzees. The team was transfixed by the lives of the chimpanzees they were filming, but a central problem remained: the film lacked a star who would lend the emotional weight an audience needs, who would make the viewers laugh and weep. And then something extraordinary happened.

The researchers and Ivorian assistants saw a baby chimp wandering through the rain forest on his own. They'd followed him since he was born and knew that he was only three years old; if he was by himself, he had to have lost his mother. It was no surprise that the baby seemed to be traumatized. Because of the lengthy bond between mothers and their infants, who are breast-fed for the first five years, no one expected the little one to survive.

Then, unusually, the little chimp started to approach the most dominant male of the group, Freddy. Freddy's behavior was incredible. The tough alpha male picked up the little scamp and cuddled him. Over the next few days, it became clear that Freddy was adopting the baby chimp. Altruism in wild animals is rare, and this case was particularly special. Freddy was not the baby's father. A magnificent animal, he's the alpha male, accustomed to controlling the group and protecting the boundary of his territory. Yet here he was playing mother to the orphan. The baby was named Oscar.

Oscar appeared worried that Freddy, like his mother, would abandon him, and he stayed close to the giant male, always touching him, never joining in play with other youngsters. Luckily, it was the coula nut season, and Freddy behaved extremely generously. Christophe exclaims, "It was an amazing sight to see this big male letting this baby pester him when he did not receive as many of the nuts as he wanted." Freddy was patient, regularly sharing his nuts; on some days, two thirds of the nuts he cracked went straight to Oscar. "Freddy was so tolerant and so caring and so attentive to Oscar. It was a beautiful relationship," comments Martyn.

But Christophe was concerned that at the end of the coula season, Oscar would deteriorate without milk or nuts. Again the chimpanzees surprised him. The team watched as Freddy opened xylia pods for the little chimp. The pods are like giant peas but when they dry out they become rock-hard, and baby chimps (who should be drinking milk) can't open them. Freddy would split them with his teeth and let Oscar eat the nutritious seeds inside. Oscar continued to gain weight and grow as Freddy shared his fruit and seeds with him. The big male carried Oscar everywhere, grooming him, looking after him, and welcoming him into his nest at night.

For directors Mark and Alastair, this was movie gold. "We instantly knew that Freddy and Oscar had the potential to be the core of the film," exudes Mark. The pair became the main storyline in the movie, and the crew looked forward to watching Oscar grow and flourish under the big male's protection. Little did the team realize how quickly the unfolding drama would be cut short.

BRUTUS

ISHA

FREDDY

Christophe unhesitatingly cites Brutus as his favorite chimp. When Christophe started his project in the 1970s, Brutus was already a mature individual and an alpha male. "He is an incredible mixture of a tough guy and a tender individual," says Christophe. "He was always the lead warrior in fights with other chimpanzee groups, very successful with females, confident, and showed the most outrageous social excitement. He's my favorite chimp because he's the chimp from which I learned the most. By watching him, I realized how complex the mind of a chimpanzee is. He represents the prototype of a chimpanzee male: on the one hand, highly aggressive; on the other, altruistic, cooperative, and supportive."

Isha was a high-ranking female, a grandmotherly figure with sun spots on her neck. She was Martyn's favorite. He thought she looked wise: "She had a sort of poise, a wonderful presence. You knew she was in control; she knew her place in the world and knew her place in the group." Martyn noticed that although she was constantly groomed by other members of the group, she rarely reciprocated. She expected to be groomed but she didn't feel obliged to return the favor!

"I was drawn to Isha very early on," Martyn recalls. "I've been lucky enough to work with many animals, including other great apes, and have made character-driven films before, so I'm used to searching out strong personalities. Isha struck me as one of these individuals. She was also happy to be filmed. She completely ignored my attention and the camera."

Martyn recalls that on his birthday, a lovely, sunny day, Isha and Oscar lay down on the forest floor and slept for much of the day. "We sat quietly with her as the sun's shadows crept across the forest floor. To be sitting with a wild chimpanzee sleeping just seven meters away was magical. She was completely at ease with us."

Oscar's adopted father is a grandfatherly figure and is Mark's favorite. Freddy has a cataract in his right eye, a slightly gray beard, and is a huge bear of a male. The dominant animal in his group, he's a lead warrior when fighting other chimp troops, yet showed a tender and caring side by looking after the orphaned Oscar so generously. Perhaps because of the cataract, he has a funny, humanlike quirk: he appears to do a double take when he sees something surprising, as if he can't quite believe what he's looking at.

PINCER

KUBA

OSCAR

There is something eye-catching about Pincer. Most chimpanzees have dark irises and no whites to their eyes; Pincer, like us, has whites. In every scene in the film, viewers can clearly see exactly where Pincer is looking. Bill, whose favorite chimp is Pincer, recalls that when he was filming chimpanzees patrolling, "Pincer would sit silently for minutes at a time, looking shiftily from left to right. It was eerie to see humanlike eyes in the face of a chimp."

Pincer is a relatively low-ranking male, yet he's fathered six children—three with a female called Kanawa and two with Kundry. This is quite rare for a chimpanzee, as males normally mate with many females. Another notable aspect about Pincer is that, despite his low status, he's a keen and adept hunter. He's also an active participant in territorial boundary patrols. Pincer's unusual eyes give him a menacing look, but he's actually a nervous, anxious chimp; he's the first to cower or sprint into a tree if another male is particularly boisterous.

Kuba is a Prince Charming, according to Ed. During filming, Kuba grew from an adolescent to a full-grown and rather handsome male and came into his own. Most chimps are recognizable by their mild imperfections, such as pigmented skin or scars; Kuba was notable for his perfect skin and fur and his symmetrical shape. If there was a fashion model among the chimp group, it would be Kuba, says Ed.

Oscar, the entire team agrees, is a charming little chimp. Heartbreakingly, Oscar lost his mother when he was three. Incredibly, alpha male Freddy adopted him. "When you look at what happened to Oscar," Christophe says, "it's easy to focus on what an extraordinary role Freddy played in the situation. But when I look at the film we shot of this odd couple, I keep thinking about how caring Freddy was about the dire fate of Oscar, and I remained impressed about his decision to help him and become his 'mother.' Oscar was just a baby, and it's unbelievable how well he coped and how determined he was. And all this despite losing his mom. I think it's the bravery and hopefulness of such a tiny little chimpanzee that makes his story so emotional."

Many Taï chimpanzees die due to disease and leopard kills. Since baby chimpanzees are entirely dependent on their mothers for a long time—five years, at least—the death of an adult female can be a tragic blow. Throughout Africa, chimps under the age of five rarely survive if their mother dies. Rubis is a typical case. When Rubis lost her mother, she slowly deteriorated. Christophe recounts, "When I saw her in the forest three months [after her mother died], she was totally alone. She was much thinner, and I could read the despair in her eyes; all interest in life had vanished. A large group of males and females joined the tree she was in, but she moved away. When they were all feeding, Rubis went even further away, utterly alone. I never saw her again."

However, to Christophe's surprise, he discovered that in the Taï forest, half of the babies that lost their moms—like little Oscar—were adopted. One day Christophe saw toddler Gia on her own. Since she was only three years old, he immediately guessed that she had lost her mother. Gia managed to survive, but injured her left arm severely enough that she was unable to move it. The outlook for Gia was bleak—but then something wonderful happened.

Porthos, an adult male, started carrying Gia on his back, as if he were a female. Whenever he sat down, Gia would sit behind him, holding on to him with one hand so that when Porthos started to move she would simply grip his shoulder and be lifted onto his back. If he walked away when she was lying on the ground, he would immediately stop at her first whimpers and bend his knees so that she could climb aboard. Christophe says, "I vividly remember seeing him making a bridge of his body to connect two trees so that Gia could easily walk on him to reach the next tree! Like a mother, Porthos was anticipating the limitations Gia would encounter due to being much smaller than him."

Gia's adoption by Porthos lasted for months; in his role as foster father he carried her for long distances, groomed her extensively, and shared his food with her. He also tenderly cared for a bad injury on her head, licking and cleaning the wounds for weeks. But Porthos, like other males, still participated in risky behavior. He went to fight neighboring groups of chimps, still carrying Gia on his back, which must have been extremely frightening for the toddler.

Sadly, when Gia was just four and a half, Porthos died from anthrax—a disease that has infected mammals in the wild for centuries, but is more commonly known now as an instrument of terrorism. Curious to discover whether or not Porthos was actually related to Gia, Christophe took a DNA sample from both chimps. His tests proved that Porthos's behavior had been completely altruistic: he was not Gia's biological father. And although their interaction was cut short, Porthos made a crucial difference in Gia's life. Christophe affirms, "To my amazement, she is still present in the group, and although she is very small in size, she is doing well."

Over the years, Christophe saw many of these adoptions and discovered that many of the foster mothers aren't mothers at all! In fact, in half the cases where babies are adopted, it is by a male. Male adoptions are unusual in most chimp populations. Freddy's adoption of Oscar seems to be evidence of the special character of the Taï chimps.

Part Three

At the end of the wet season, in October 2010, after two years of filming in the Ivory Coast, the crew was scheduled to fly back to the U.K. The plan was to rest and recuperate, then return in 2011 for a final four-month stint. The camp was in a state of excitement as the crew packed up: the first democratic election to be held in the Ivory Coast in years was to take place in November. Cooks Grand Alain and Petit Alain spent hours debating which party would be better for the country and their village.

A month later, after the crew was safely back home, the election took place. The sitting president, Laurent Gbagbo, was defeated and challenged the results. The UN, backed by the international community, stepped in and declared the opposition leader, Alassane Ouattara, the winner, but Gbagbo would not stand down. The country was on the verge of civil war. Fighting broke out, and 3,000 people were killed.

Back in Bristol, England, the team listened with trepidation as they learned that most of the violent outbreaks were in towns they knew well—places they relied on for supplies and staff. In one of the nearest villages to the camp, Ponan, old tribal feuds broke out, and some of the assistants living there had to flee across the border to Liberia. Memories of the recent civil war were still fresh, and many of the Ivorians were terrified that the country was going to go to war again.

Alastair and Mark decided that it was too dangerous for the crew to return. The researchers on the Taï chimp project were forced to evacuate. For the first time in thirty years, no one was with the chimps of the Taï forest.

RIGHT: Field producer James Reed (left) and cameraman Warwick Sloss film on an inselberg in Minkebe National Park, Gabon.

Despite this devastating blow, the film still had to be finished. There were crucial scenes and shots that Mark and Alastair needed, and they had planned to have a dedicated shoot to film the forest itself—to obtain beautiful images of the world in which the chimps live, which was not easy to do when following the chimps on the ground. Since the team was unable to return to the Ivory Coast, the only option was to find a similar rain forest in a neighboring country.

The problem was that many of the Ivory Coast's neighbors are also politically unstable or, like Ghana, peaceful but depleted of forest. After much debate, the team chose Gabon, as it's a safe location and has some of the most beautiful and pristine jungle left in the world. But choosing a country that has a tiny population, is mostly covered with forest, and was only recently mapped, would be a challenge.

Over the course of several trips, the crew spent a total of eight weeks filming in Gabon. But one trip proved to be especially taxing. The idea was to film from an inselberg—a steep-sided granite outcrop that towers over the rain forest and would give the crew a much-needed vantage point. However, the inselberg was almost five hundred miles away from the nearest road, and few people had been there. Mark and Alastair felt that the only practical way to get there with film equipment was to fly by helicopter.

In March 2011, Ed, James, cameraman Warwick Sloss, and two eco-guards flew to Minkebe, in Gabon. The helicopter safely deposited them on the tip of the inselberg, but the pilot was loath to switch off his engine, pointing out that they were more than five hundred miles from rescue if there were a problem. The team jumped out with all their equipment and waved good-bye to the pilot—and as soon as the helicopter was out of sight, their problems began.

African honeybees descended on the men in alarmingly large numbers. Soon they were covered in bees. At first, although disconcerted, the filmmakers found it quite amusing. The bees didn't sting, but instead concentrated on licking sweaty patches on the men's bodies. But toward the end of the day, the bees began to attack.

When a bee stings, it releases an odor that signals to other bees that it is under attack. This attracts more bees to the source of the threat. So after a few stings, more and more bees arrived, behaving far more aggressively than they had earlier.

By dusk, everyone had been stung at least fifty times. The cumulative effect was not something any of them had experienced before. "The acute

pain is very stressful," says James, "but so is the anticipation of being stung. You panic—it's a pain that you can't ignore—and waiting to be stung again ruins your concentration."

That evening, the team put up their tents and built a fire. They were huddled around it, feeling depressed and worried, when suddenly the earth shook and knocked them all to the ground. "We screamed and panicked," says James. A few moments later, there was a mighty thunderclap, followed by torrential rain. "It dawned on us—we'd been struck by lightning!" exclaims James. A bolt of lightning had hit a tree next to their tents, and the electricity had spread through the root system, electrocuting them from beneath the ground. "We ran blindly into the forest to get away from the tree," says James, "and crouched in the jungle, wet, cold, and miserable while we waited for the storm to pass."

The following morning, after a fitful night's sleep, the team was still recovering from the shock. They rose at five to film the sunrise. Mist lay wreathed across the canopy below them, the forest stretching endless and unbroken as far as the horizon. The sky was clear, and in one of the most beautiful places on earth, it felt like a fresh start. But as soon as the sun rose, the bees returned. They arrived quickly, in far greater numbers than the day before, and stung as soon as they landed on the men. "Our stress levels soared," recalls James. "Plus, it's very difficult to operate a camera with bees crawling into your eyes and mouth and stinging repeatedly."

The team made one of their hardest calls—for the helicopter to come back and rescue them. They knew that Alastair and Mark, having spent a substantial amount of money on a thousand-mile round trip to film a crucial scene, would not be pleased. "What was a great relief, though," says James, "was that we didn't come back empty-handed. We shot a perfect sunrise and the most atmospheric misty forest shots—like something out of *Jurassic Park* or *Avatar*—that you could possibly hope for."

"We wanted to transport the audience to the middle of a West African rain forest so they could feel what it's like to be in the heart of the chimpanzees' world," maintains Mark. Which is a difficult feat, because showing the forest in two dimensions on a television or cinema screen renders it flat and lifeless. To give depth to the jungle, the camera needs to move. Flying a camera over the forest isn't difficult: previous crews have used a helicopter. But the closer the helicopter is to the canopy, the more the downdraft from the blades shakes the leaves.

In the past, Mark and Alastair had managed to get low-level images of the canopy by using a hot air balloon modified for filming, but they quickly realized that such a contraption wasn't going to work in this part of Gabon because there were no good places to take off or land. "Instead, we had to fly the camera through the upper layer of the canopy using cables," recounts Mark. To do this, they turned to Ted Giffords and his colleagues Tim Fogg and James Aldred, expert climbers who were able to rig the trees and pull cables between them. The camera was then suspended from the steel cables in a cradle called a dolly. To stop the camera from twisting and rocking, Ted stabilized the dolly with two spinning, copper-wrapped bicycle wheels. "It was a real Rube Goldberg contraption, but amazingly effective when working well," says Mark.

The device was as quirky in operation as it was in appearance, and weeks passed before the crew was happy with the results, but eventually their patience was rewarded, and they were able to film stunning shots of the West African rain forest.

NEAR LEFT: Cameraman Warwick Sloss (standing at the base of the tree), Tim Fogg (the climber in red), and Ted Giffords (operating the camera) rig a camera on cables to film the canopy in Gabon.

Throughout the three years that the crew had been traveling back and forth to the Ivory Coast, cameraman Bill Wallauer and his wife, fellow chimp expert and sound recordist Kristin Mosher, had been traveling to and from Uganda to film the rivals—the Ngogo chimpanzees in Kibale National Park (see "Kibale National Park" sidebar). The Ngogo chimps have been studied since 1995 by primatologists John Mitani from the University of Michigan and David Watts from Yale University. These chimps are unusual because they live in an exceptionally large group—more than 160 individuals, with over thirty adult males. So many males means there are high levels of ape warfare.

Like some human tribes, chimpanzees wage orchestrated battles against neighboring groups (see "War!" sidebar). In the tangled vegetation of Taï, it was hard to film such fights, but in Kibale, with its pockets of semi-open woodland, tropical rain forest, and savannah, it was a little easier. Bill, who is the official wildlife cameraman for the Jane Goodall Institute, has spent most of his time with the chimpanzees of Gombe, Tanzania. He recalls, "From the moment I entered the forests of Ngogo, I knew I was in a special place. There were fig trees whose branches were bigger than some of the largest trees in Gombe, massive swamps, and herds of elephant and buffalo. Even more amazing was the number of chimps. The rich habitat and amount of fruit means there are three times as many chimps than in any other site in Africa. To me this was incredible; the group of chimps I follow in Tanzania has only twelve males."

Over the past eighteen years, Bill has witnessed many territorial patrols, but he was astounded by the chimpanzee behavior at Ngogo. Shortly after he arrived, he witnessed one of the most dramatic chimp wars he'd ever seen. Between twenty and thirty males were moving silently through the forest. Bill kept running on ahead and circling them. Finally, he got the shot he wanted. The group he was following met their enemies and Bill captured the exact moment. "A distant call from the rival chimps broke the silence. The males were coming right toward me, looking directly into the camera. The males at the front of the patrol all stood up bipedally and erected their hair so that they looked twice as big."

On another occasion, he was with a relatively small group of Ngogo males. It was clear that one of them had heard something to the south, almost certainly an enemy patrol. "We crept slowly through the vegetation, frequently stopping to listen," says Bill. "The six or seven males I was with were taking a huge risk. If they were outnumbered, one of them could have been caught and killed."

A young male called Dexter was in front; Pincer and some of the older, more experienced males were at the back. "As Kristin and I moved up a steep hill in the direction we had last seen Dexter, all hell broke loose," Bill remembers. "Earsplitting screams erupted all around us. We were surrounded by black, charging blurs." The Ngogo males realized they were outnumbered and tried to retreat. "I will never forget the moment that Dexter burst out of the thicket in front of me with a huge enemy male in pursuit," says Bill. "The dark black face and white beard of the aggressor is etched in my mind. When he saw us, he stopped in his tracks and fled. We had almost certainly saved Dexter's life."

For chimpanzees, defending home territory can be incredibly dangerous, if not deadly. The males of a community must work silently and systematically as they search for signs of intruders in their own area or trespass into the territory of a rival community. When an enemy is encountered, decisions must be made quickly and decisively; inexperience can be fatal. "The key to success is clearly numerical superiority," says Bill, "but courage, experience, and confidence also play a vital role. It sounds as if I am describing human guerrilla warfare! But there are astonishing similarities between our two species: the tactics during these military-like patrols by chimpanzees mirror the behavior of a well-trained combat unit."

Kibale Park is in southwest Uganda, just north of the equator. It was created in 1993 and is home to over three hundred species of birds and several species of large mammals, such as elephant, buffalo, and giant forest hog. Researchers observe twelve types of primates at Kibale, including red colobus monkeys. Ugandan scientist Isabirye Basuta began to study the chimpanzees in 1976. Today, three communities of chimps are "habituated"—meaning they are accustomed to people following them. Two, Kanyawara and Ngogo, are studied by scientists, and the third, Kanyanchu, is visited by tourists.

WAR!

Chimpanzees, like many animals, are highly territorial. One reason for this behavior may be that male chimps stay where they were born, while females travel to live in new groups. Since the males are surrounded by the chimpanzees they grew up with, they develop strong bonds with their friends and relatives and are keen to have a large territory that will attract females. The difference between chimpanzees and other animals (apart from humans!) is the lengths to which they'll go to defend or expand their territory. Male chimpanzees work as a team, sometimes killing other chimps during these territorial battles. Although the Taï chimpanzees do have territorial fights, they are often less violent than those seen in Ngogo. The Taï chimps regularly rush to support outnumbered group members, which makes deadly attacks much less likely.

Chimp warfare starts off with a patrol. While on patrol, chimpanzees move in single file to the periphery of their territory. When they reach the boundary, they fall silent and begin to scan their enemies' territory. They are attentive to every sound and startle at the slightest movement or noise. Occasionally, patrollers make deep incursions into their neighbors' land.

At Ngogo, around thirteen males, like Pincer, Scar, and Mweya, patrol every couple of weeks. About half the time, they meet their neighbors, and a shouting match ensues. This usually doesn't lead to physical confrontation, but sometimes the patrollers launch a lethal attack. This normally happens when one group of patrolling chimps greatly outnumbers a rival group. The males use their numerical superiority to subdue and kill their foes. Assaults only last a few minutes, but victims are bitten, brutally beaten, and kicked so badly they frequently die from massive internal injuries.

"Lethal attacks are the most dramatic events in the lives of chimpanzees," explains primatologist John Mitani. "They're quick and chaotic and the noise created by chimpanzees, who scream as they maul their victims, is deafening. They're a normal part of the behavioral repertoire of chimpanzees, but the need for scientific objectivity does not make them any less gruesome or easy to watch."

In May 2011, the situation in the Ivory Coast stabilized after Alassane Ouattara, who had won the 2010 election, was inaugurated as president. Civil war was averted, and the film crew was able to return to Taï. Throughout this period, Christophe had been fighting for the survival of the Taï chimps, worried that without the presence of the researchers and assistants, the camp would be looted and the apes killed. A few weeks after the election, he'd been able to reach some of the field assistants, who returned to their post. As the situation improved, a few of the researchers joined them. Everyone was hugely relieved to learn that all the chimps had survived. It's a happy ending, but serves to highlight how precarious the position of the chimpanzees is.

All wild chimpanzees live in Africa, and many of the countries where they're found are politically unstable and impoverished. Chimps are frequently hunted and killed for meat, and their forests are logged for tropical hardwoods. They suffer from the same diseases as us and are capable of catching respiratory infections from humans, which almost invariably kill them. The forests are reservoirs for the Ebola virus and anthrax, diseases that have decimated the apes. As a result, the chimps are highly endangered; they've been wiped out in a number of countries, and scientists believe they are on the brink of extinction.

Several years ago, Christophe witnessed an incident that serves to highlight how complex the situation is. "I remember very vividly the day I was following a group of chimpanzees moving along a ridge in the forest in the middle of the dry season," he says. "The dead leaves on the forest floor were so desiccated, we rustled as we walked. A group of chimps was resting on the ground, and the kids were playing in tangled vines. I knew all these youngsters, and I noticed that a very playful adolescent female was sitting quietly next to them instead of joining in. What had happened to Fédora? Normally she was always right in the center of any play session."

Fédora turned around, and Christophe saw to his horror that three of her fingers were so badly damaged that he could see her bones. Then he noticed that a cable was wrapped around her right hand, cutting straight through her fingers. The young chimp must have fallen into a snare trap in one of the illegal cocoa bean fields within the park. Farmers protect their fields using snare traps made from bicycle brake cables. Usually they trap antelope in them, which they eat to supplement their meager diet, but sadly, many chimpanzees are caught in the snares, too. Adult chimpanzees are clever enough to remove the cables, but youngsters are not, and as they're so afraid of the pain, they refuse to let the older chimps help them.

Fédora was in agony and certainly not in the mood to play. "Stupidly, I asked myself, 'Why her?'" says Christophe. "I had followed her since she was born, and now I was there to see her die in agony." Over the next few days, Fédora lost one finger bone at a time. Eventually her whole hand came off and with it, the snare. This excruciatingly painful wound took six months to heal. But to Christophe's delight, the old, playful Fédora resurfaced. She became a keen tool user, learning to pound nuts with her left hand. "Whenever I saw her, I smiled," recounts Christophe, "at the joy for life she had regained since the terrible trauma she'd undergone."

When she was ten, Fédora vanished completely. Christophe was pleased. Since chimpanzee females leave to join another chimp group when they become sexually active, Fédora must have felt strong enough to risk the adventure.

The Taï chimpanzees now effectively live on an island—a forested island surrounded by an ever-growing, poverty-stricken human population. "We are transforming protected areas into islands, and all wild animals suffer from the competition for land and water that drives humans ever closer to these wild, pristine areas," Christophe says. "The only hope for nature and wild animals is that we actively preserve them by creating enough protected areas."

Fédora may by now be a mother of two in a new group and, if undisturbed, will thrive. All chimpanzees, including the stars of the film— Freddy, Oscar, Zyon, and their friends and family—are dependent on the goodwill of humans for their survival. Christophe and the film crew hope the movie *Chimpanzee* will not only entertain audiences for years to come, but also encourage everyone to preserve our planet's wonderful forests and our closest cousins.

What You Can Do

- Support conservation projects such as the Wild Chimpanzee Foundation (wildchimps.org), which has been working with Taï National Park and local populations for years.

- Support chimpanzee protection and local communities in Africa through organizations such as the Jane Goodall Institute (janegoodall.org).

- Buy coffee, cocoa, and soap that have been produced without cutting down rain forest.

- Don't buy biofuel grown on land that was once pristine forest.

- Buy tropical hardwoods from sustainable sources (such as those with the Forest Stewardship Council label).

— Acknowledgments —

*F*irst and foremost, we would like to thank our chimpanzee stars, without whom neither the movie nor the book would have been possible. We have no idea whether they miss us, but we miss them.

Without chimpanzees that are habituated to the presence of humans, an established camp in the jungle, and trained field assistants, our job would have been impossible. It takes many people to run a research camp in a remote African forest and we owe a debt to them all. The Taï forest research station in the Ivory Coast is run by the Max Planck Institute for Evolutionary Anthropology and Department of Primatology, Leipzig, Germany. Many students of all nationalities offered their time, knowledge, and good company; among them were Livia Wittiger, Lydia Luncz, Nadin Eckhardt, Sonja Metzger, Lissa Ongman, Genevieve Campbell, Ammie Kalan, Karline Janmaat, Alexandra Guignard, and Danielle Spitzer. From our team, Hugh Wilson was a valuable field assistant on the first shoot. Without the constant financial support of first the Swiss National Science Foundation and then the Max Planck Society, the Taï chimpanzee project would not exist and the film would not have been possible.

The film crew relied heavily on local Ivorians. Quasimodo de Ponan and his team—Leon, Nicaise, and Fal—helped to construct our camp in the middle of the forest. Once building was complete, Alain Toubate became our camp cook and assistant, and his culinary skills developed considerably during the production (thankfully). Alain was ably assisted by Jean-Claude Blaihyo. While filming, Valentine Yagnon, Arsene Sioblo, and Alphonse Tagnon helped track our subjects and carry the brutally heavy equipment. Thanks also to Charlie Hubert Biorou, Nestor Gouyan Bah, Olivier Dehegnan, Apollinaire Gnahe Djirian, Jonas Mompeho Tahou, Florent Goulei, and Alain Takouo for their forest skills. Sidiki Kone and Philbert Gbleu were always reliable drivers. And a big thank you to the villages of Taï, Gouleako, Pauleoula, Doubly, and Ponan for the help given to the film crew and the Taï Chimpanzee Project over the years.

Permission to film in the forest was granted by colonel Kahiba Lambert and his team at the Office Ivoirien des Parcs et Réserves, with local help from lieutenants Kramo and Yao and their many guards at L'Office des Eaux et Forêts. Thanks are also due to the staff at the Taï National Park office.

In Abidjan, the Centre Suisse de Recherches Scientifiques was an invaluable port in the storm from which we organized our travels and received logistical help. Special thanks to Gueladio Cisse and Bassirou Bonfoh. At the offices of the Wild Chimpanzee Foundation, Ilka Herbinger and Dervla

Dowd were very generous with their time and knowledge, helping us on numerous occasions.

At the start of production, the Ivory Coast had just emerged from a period of civil war, and trouble threatened to return several times during the production. Advice was always at hand from Paul Kelly, Linda Reid, and Mark Kroeker in The Walt Disney Company's security section and also from the U.S. embassy in Abidjan. Monica Mark and Tim Cox gave us constant updates from the ground during the worst periods, and during our final trip, Abdoul Wahabou Sall and the United Nations Mission in the Ivory Coast advised and escorted our team. Thank you to all.

A final note of thanks to Craig Hitchcock and the friendly and ever-helpful Sue Hogwood of the British Foreign Office. Sue sadly died of malaria in March 2010.

UGANDA

Uganda was home to our rival group of chimpanzees, and we are extremely grateful to John Mitani and David Watts for allowing us to share their study site. We are also indebted to the project director, Jeremiah Lwanga, and the many students who provided information on chimpanzee movements and tolerated our film equipment strewn around their camp, particularly Lauren Sarringhaus, Kevin Langergraber, James Fenton, and Michelle Brown.

The field assistants from Makerere University Biological Field Station helped to track the chimpanzees and carry equipment. We are very grateful to all of them: Adolph Magoba, Alfred Tumusiime, Godfrey Mbabazi, Lawrence Ndangizi, Ambrozio Twineomujuni, Charles William Ddumba, James Tibisimwa, James Zahura, Richard Nyakahuma, and Charles Birungi. Charles Businge and Annette Akugizibwe helped run the camp and cook.

We were allowed to enter the Ngogo region of Kibale National Park with the kind permission of the Uganda Wildlife Authority and the Media Council. The Jane Goodall Institute in Entebbe provided invaluable logistical support and stored much of our equipment between trips. Special thanks to Debby Cox, Dr. Panta Kasoma, and Mary-Lou Allen.

The Gately Inn was our ever-friendly hotel of choice. Thanks to all the staff for making our travels more enjoyable.

Finally, we would like to remember Cliff Kisitu, our transportation manager, chief driver, and loyal friend, who tragically died in a boating accident shortly after we completed filming. Cliff was passionate about chimpanzees and his homeland. He was loved by many people and will be greatly missed, especially by his adoring family.

GABON

The beautiful country of Gabon served to provide our West African rain forest scenery when the Ivory Coast became too dangerous. Immense thanks to Lee White, Josh Ponte, Christian Tchemambela, and all the staff at the Agence Nationale des Parcs Nationaux who did so much to help us achieve our goals. If similar organizations in Africa could emulate their drive and commitment, the continent's wildlife would have a brighter future. For the helicopter aerials the Gendarmerie Nationale, République Gabonaise, and the team of captain Ella Nkoulou Jean Jacques were tireless and very patient. Thank you to David Baillie for rigging the helicopter and to Michael Kelem, our aerial cameraman. Daniel Mulligan provided invaluable assistance on technical aspects of the shoot.

Our thanks to all those who helped us film in the Forets Classée de Munda, Belinga Mountain, and the national parks of Ivindo and Minkébé. A special thank you goes to Joseph Okouyi, based in Mokokou, and the many others too numerous to mention. Gabon was also the scene of our rope-dolly filming, where a camera was flown within the forest on a cable. This is never an easy undertaking, but James Aldred, Ted Giffords, and Tim Fogg worked nonstop and with great skill to make this part of the shoot a success. Warwick Sloss was the cameraman on this shoot—thank you for maintaining good humor in the face of stinging bees and lightning strikes on the camp. Finally, Tim Shepherd, our time-lapse photography maestro, also needed good humor and plenty of patience to film fungi and plants growing.

ENGLAND AND THE UNITED STATES

Back in Bristol, England, Sarah Garner offered production support from the office, and production accountant Rachel James kept the money on track. Films@59, run by Gina Fucci and George Panayiotou, was our home in the U.K., and we consider everyone who works there as part of the team. Special thanks to Gordon Leicester and his crew in the hire department, who maintained our equipment and gave us great advice at all times of the day and night, often via satellite phone, while we were on location. Dan Clamp delivered an extraordinary blend of knowledge and hard work to keep our technology running smoothly throughout the production.

The greatest debt of thanks must go to Jean-Francois Camilleri, who created Disneynature shortly before commissioning *Chimpanzee*. Needless to say, the movie could not have happened without him. "JF" has been available with support—creative and financial—at every stage of production, and his contribution to the film has been immense. Alan Bergman, president of the Walt Disney Studios, has been a loyal supporter throughout, and Don Hahn, our executive producer, offered superb creative advice from the early stages.

Alix Tidmarsh, with her considerable knowledge of the film industry, helped us to navigate the complex world of contracts and budgets so we could secure the resources we needed. Keith Scholey endured more screenings of our early cuts than anyone else and offered valuable advice, for which we are most grateful.

The whole team at Disneynature has been fantastic, with special mentions going to Sten Jorgensen, Fanny Gire, Matthew Scholey, Catherine Stephens, and Paul Baribault, along with Beth Stevens and Kim Sams of the conservation team.

Last but not least is the fantastic team at Disney Editions. Many thanks to Jessie Ward, Wendy Lefkon, Jennifer Eastwood, Marybeth Tregarthen, Gregory Lauzon, Warren Meislin, Nancy Inteli, and Hannah Buchsbaum. A special thanks to designer Stuart Smith and illustrator Jean-Paul Orpiñas, whose contributions to the visual quality of this book are greatly appreciated. Thanks also to Stephen Johnson, who graded the photographs quickly and expertly.